Meteor Attack!

Neutrinoman & Lightningirl
A Love Story

Episode #1

Robert J. McCarter

Little Hummingbird Publishing
Flagstaff, AZ

Meteor Attack!
Neutrinoman & Lightningirl: A Love Story, Episode #1

Cover images (Earth and asteroid) courtesy of NASA's Visible Earth: visibleearth.nasa.gov

Version 1.2, July 2014
Version 1.1, July 2013
Version 1.0, April 2012
ISBN: 978-0-9642096-6-4

Find out more about this series at: Neutrinoman.com
Visit Robert's website at: RobertJMcCarter.com

 Published by:
Little Hummingbird Publishing
P.O. Box 23518
Flagstaff, AZ 86002
www.LittleHummingbird.com

Little Hummingbird Publishing is a division of Arapas, Inc. Find more about Arapas at: www.Arapas.com.

Dedicated to my beautiful wife Aleia. I always wanted to experience a great and epic love, and with her I have just that. Our twenty-plus years together have been all that I could have hoped for and more.

Prologue

Spring 2025, Casita de Soledad, Central Arizona

"So?" I asked her, my eyes taunting her, daring her. "Where should I start?"

Her brown eyes wandered before meeting mine, her shoulders shrugging as she said, "Well, if you must do this, start at the most important part."

We stood in the living room of our little adobe casita, the high-desert sunset bathing her beautiful face in golden light. After all these years I was a happy man just staring at her.

"The origin story?" I said. "How we became superheroes? That's it. How it really all began, not the PR-scrubbed version that everyone knows."

She shook her head, her long black hair gliding back and forth across her shoulders. "No, no. Those stories are good and heroic, and close enough. Everyone knows them, start at the most important part."

I had the feeling I was being tested. It wasn't the first time she made me feel that way (not by a long shot), nor the last.

"Uhh," I said, my index finger pointing heavenward. "The

climactic battle when we defeated the Arcturian Alliance, and then go backwards from there. That is—"

"Not the most important part," she said, cutting me off. She walked over, her hand resting gently on my chest, the yellow and white tendrils of energy arcing back and forth as our bodies did their dance. I felt the electrical tingle I had felt since the first time we had touched. It still thrilled me each and every time.

I nodded my head and smiled, she followed suit. "The most important part is..." I began, watching her right eyebrow arch. "The most important part is... it's..." Suddenly I knew what it was and I knew what kind of story I was going to write. "It's when we met," I said with a smile.

She smiled wide and full, rewarding me with the grace of her pleasure. "That's my man, my Neutrinoman," she said, invoking an old ritual between us.

"That's my girl, my Lightningirl," I replied, sweeping her up into my arms, feeling electricity course through me as I carried her towards the bedroom. She giggled a girlish giggle, and my writing was forgotten for the day.

Before that moment I knew this was a story of superheroes and cataclysmic events, a story of aliens and war, of change and human fallibility. But that one moment with her, with my love, made it clear that this was to be—first and foremost—a love story.

Chapter 1

The Setup

Fall 2004, Buckeye, Arizona

MY NAME IS NIK NICHOLS AND I AM NEUTRINOMAN. You know: mild-mannered janitor at the Palo Verde Nuclear Generating Station by day, Neutrinoman by night. *Radiating our way to a better tomorrow.*

Her name is Licia Lopez and she is Lightningirl. I know. I know. Why is the male superhero a "man" and the female superhero a "girl"? I asked her about it once and she said, "Yeah, I used to hate it, but now that I am over thirty, I kinda like it, actually."

Where was I... Oh yeah... She is Lightningirl: mild-mannered Arizona Public Service (APS) lineman (line-*woman* as she calls it) by day, Lightningirl by night. *Electrifying our lives.*

You've heard how it all happened, on that full moon day in 2003 when the world was awash in cosmic rays. When the accident at Palo Verde occurred and I went into the reactor and opened the stuck valve on the emergency cooling system, exposing me to a deadly dose of radiation. And how, as I lay there dying, that golden-hued, neutrino-mutated rat took a big bite out of my leg, and with help from the cosmic rays, mutated my DNA and turned me into: Neutrinoman.

And you've heard how on that same fateful day she was repairing high-tension power lines near Flagstaff, trying to restore power to half of Arizona, when she was struck by lightning and thrown onto an open transformer. How, as she lay there dying, the mutated raven pecked on her hand, and with help from the cosmic rays, transformed her DNA and turned her into: Lightningirl.

Well, there are some things that need to be set straight. The origin stories, considering the PR machine they went through, are close enough. But there are some parts of our stories that have never been told, some wrongs that need to be righted, and there are some details you just won't believe. And now that we are both retired, and out of the game, I can tell you. Finally.

How, before the public knew very much about us, how Lightningirl and Neutrinoman met, and fell in love, and—

But I am getting ahead of myself, aren't I?

It all began in Buckeye, Arizona, at my parents' house about one year after the accident. I was still working as a janitor at Palo Verde and not making very much money. I was living at home, and my mom had invited some friends from Flagstaff over for dinner. The Lopez family. I suspected a setup; my mom was always doing that.

"A setup, what do you mean a setup?" she asked when I casually brought it up. I was setting the dining room table—the good china was out—while she was in the kitchen, with her head in the oven, poking at the roast.

"The Lopezes have a daughter, right? And she is about thirty, about my age, right?" Mom hmmm-hmmmed from the oven. "And she is single, right?"

Her head out of the oven, she said, "So what is so wrong with that? I can't invite friends over for dinner that happen to have a single daughter your age?"

"And how well do you know them?"

"We sat next to them at the Cardinals game last month."

"So not at all, then," I said.

"They seemed so nice, no harm in getting to know them."

"It's a setup, Mom, why can't you just admit that?"

She came out of the kitchen wiping her hands on her apron, and placed her left hand on my chest. "I just want to see my son happy. All these years since that Ashley girl broke your heart and here you are still single."

My jaw bunched at the mention of Ashley, but I didn't say anything. I looked at her. She had blond hair this year in waves down to her shoulders. She was plump and matronly in her early fifties with plenty of makeup on. The new hair color still threw me, but her brown eyes were as deep and as kind as ever. The same brown eyes I had, the same brown eyes that had first caught Ashley's attention. She meant well, she always meant well, it was just complicated.

"Mom, I am not in a good position for a relationship right now. Since the accident, I—"

"I am so tired of hearing about that accident. My boy, he talks to the president, but can't tell anyone what amazing things he does. All the lives he saves. Well, if Mister President ever comes over for dinner, I'll have a thing or two to—"

The doorbell rang, cutting her off. "Al," she yelled to my father, "it's the Lopezes. Can you get that?" She turned back to me, fooled with my collar, and said, "You look handsome, Nik. She's a nice girl. I think you'll like her."

I frowned at her. The last thing I wanted was romantic complications.

"Just give it a chance," she said with a smile. "For your mother."

I GUESS, STRICTLY SPEAKING, I DIDN'T HAVE TO LIVE AT home. And I'm not sure if that makes it more or less lame. It's clichéd (a thirty-year-old man living at home) and I know it, but you know what? I have great parents, and I had a great childhood. I don't have horrible traumas in my past to explain it or deep psychological scars to fall back on. At that point in my life, it made more sense to save what money I could and live with them instead of saving no money and living in a crap apartment.

I know, I know. Thirty and a janitor. Well, believe me, I didn't plan for it to go that way. I just wasn't one of those driven people. I never felt the need to change the world, or prove myself, or any of that. I made it through college and just kind of floated. I could certainly have gotten a better job than janitor, but I was working at Palo Verde because I wanted to. I would have taken something else, but that was the first job I could land that got me in the door.

What can I say? I was curious about the power plant and wanted to learn about it and see the inside. So I figured out a way to do that and get paid at the same time.

It was kind of a pain back then, though. You wouldn't think Neutrinoman would still need to hold down a day job, but the Feds wanted to keep things quiet. That, and my need to have access to the radiation, kept me there.

And I guess me being Neutrinoman is the crux of it. I wasn't living at home at the time of the accident, but after it happened I moved back home. Mom and Dad know about what happened to me, and I have found that I need people around me who know the truth. I just can't keep a secret like that all the time.

So, yeah, I'm sure it *looked* lame, but it was the best thing for me.

LICIA LOPEZ WAS A PETITE LATINA, WITH MODERATE curves, a round face, jet black hair, and soft brown eyes. I can't say I could argue with my mother's taste, in this case.

I carefully shook hands with Elena and John Lopez first. I took great care, as I always did, when making physical contact to ensure that I was fully in my biological form. Elena's hand was small and soft, her grip light. John's hand was calloused and his grip strong.

"And this is our daughter Licia," John said with a Mexican accent his daughter did not share. I reached out and took her hand, shaking it, and felt an electrical shock.

"Ow!" I said, rather involuntarily.

She pulled her hand back when I did, looking at it like she felt something too. "I'm sorry," Licia said, "I am just a magnet for static electricity."

I smiled, but something wasn't right. She had just shaken both of my parents' hands and there hadn't been any shocks. Something was going on.

AFTER WE HAD EATEN, EVERYONE WAS CHATTING IN THE living room, the fathers were discussing sports, and the mothers were discussing—well, I don't know what they were discussing, I couldn't follow it. I do know it involved shoes.

I hadn't gotten much out of Licia. She worked for APS as a linewoman, lived in Flagstaff, and was a rock climber. She was very restrained in her answers, but not in a shy way.

Anyway, after we had all eaten, I went back to the adjoining dining room and started gathering plates up.

"I'll help," Licia said, grabbing an armload of plates like a pro.

"You've done this before," I said in the kitchen.

"Waitress."

I nodded. I put everything in the sink, poked my head out and saw the folks were deep in conversation. Licia was going back for more when I whispered, "Hold up."

She threw me a questioning look so I said, "Let the older generation bond. Besides, I have a question for you."

She shrugged her shoulders, "Okay, what is it?"

"Umm... this is going to sound weird." She just stared. "Do you mind if we shake hands again?"

"It was nothing. I told you I have static electricity problems." Her downcast brown eyes were avoiding mine as she turned to go.

"Please."

"Why is this so important to you?"

"I... I can't say, not yet."

She turned around again, and I reached out a finger to touch her exposed arm.

As my finger approached, I saw blue-white sparks arc from her skin to my finger while yellow sparks flew from my skin to hers. She spun around, breaking the near contact, her eyes wild.

"Don't touch me. Ever."

Chapter 2

Dads and Dates
Fall 2004, Buckeye, Arizona

You KNOW HOW IN THOSE SAPPY ROMANCES THE SOON TO be lovers always describe their first touch as "electric"? Well, I never expected it to be *literally* electric. I saw the spark of electricity travel from her to me. I saw my own body react. I felt the energy travel up my arm. It was real. I felt it, and I know she felt it too.

I didn't know what to make of it. The sensation wasn't entirely comfortable, but I longed to experience it again.

Now, you're a savvy reader. You know who she is. But at the time, I had no clue. All I knew was that I had just met a beautiful woman that affected me physically in a way I had never experienced before.

"You're awfully quiet, son," Mom said. We all sat in the living room reading. Our nineteen-sixties era ranch-style house is mostly my mother's domain. The living room has lots of figurines and doilies, shag carpet in shades of brown far past its prime, a couch and two La-Z-Boys, and reproductions of serine Thomas Kinkade style landscapes.

Dad was scouring a catalog of vintage car parts. Mom

was reading *The Da Vinci Code*. And I was pretending to read a textbook on nuclear physics.

"Umm—" I began.

My dad saved me. He got up and said to her, "Can't you see the boy is thinking?" My dad is just an average guy, kind of like me: brown hair, brown eyes, medium build. Middle age has brought a thinning of his hair up top, some grey, and a bulging around the gut—also quite average.

In retrospect it is obvious who Licia was, right? Well, that is retrospect for you, not reality; right then and there, I didn't have a clue.

After that dinner with the Lopezes, my life continued its normal, and very odd, pattern: working at Palo Verde (very boring) and doing the superhero gig (very exciting). But amidst it all I kept thinking about her.

After stopping the bank robbery and freeing the hostages at the main Wells Fargo branch, I thought of her. After keeping the Ferris wheel from collapsing and saving hundreds of lives at the Arizona State Fair, I thought of her. After emptying the trash and polishing the floors at the Palo Verde Nuclear Generating Station, I thought of her. After eating my mom's meatloaf, I thought of her.

And this was a bit surprising. There had been girls since Ashley, but it had been casual and I had never been engaged like this. It was getting ridiculous. Seriously. Even my dad noticed, and that's saying something.

"Come on, son," he said after putting his catalog away. "I need some help with the Charger."

"Al," Mom started, "no use of powers. You know the rules."

"Of course not," he answered, grinning at me.

He led me out to the double garage, which held his prized

possession: a black, 1972 Dodge Charger. He was "restoring" it. Actually, he had been restoring it since I was ten. It was not clear to any of us (I think Dad included) why it was taking so long.

The garage is my father's domain. It's neat as a pin, full of tools, everything clean and orderly. My dad was an accountant, but he tinkered with cars on the weekends. He had this white-collar side (work and making money) and this blue-collar side (cars, football, Coors beer, and Bruce Springsteen).

"I need a weld," he said. "The metal is starting to crack around the driver's-side door hinge. It's gonna break eventually."

I nodded and went over to look. The garage was brutally hot (but only brutally, it was fall in the Valley of the Sun, after all). Dad cracked the garage door and moved the portable air conditioner in place to blow on us. He also clipped a light to the door and rigged it to shine on the hinge.

It was a hairline crack running the length of one side of the hinge. I took a deep breath and concentrated on the tip of my right index finger, willing it—and just it—to go neutrino. Slowly my flesh transformed into the pulsing, glowing yellow of my neutrino form.

While I did my transformation, Dad put some blocks under the open car door, taking the weight off it.

This was harder than a complete transformation, but safer for everyone, and everything, around me. Once the tip of my finger was a bright yellow, like the sun, with swirls and motes running through it, Dad handed me a thin dowel of steel.

I rubbed my finger along the crack until the metal started glowing red. I then scraped small amounts of metal off the rod and worked them into the crack. With my finger all neutrino, it was like working with Play-Doh. I went slowly and carefully and soon the crack was filled, and the metal was cooling.

I sat back on the cement and let the cool air flow over me.

My dad handed me a beer, sat down next to me and said, "Good job, son. So, shall we talk about her?"

You know what strikes horror into a superhero's heart? Not the League of Villains, Extraordinaire (LoVE) not the Arcturian Alliance, not Toxicwasteman, nope, none of those. What strikes horror into this superhero's heart is talking with his father about his romantic feelings.

My dad is a good, kind man. I know he cares for me and my mother deeply, but he's not the warm-fuzzy kind.

When he handed me the beer, his face was his usual stony mask as he ran his fingers through his thinning brown hair.

We weren't done with the door yet. We had to wait for the metal to cool and try it out, make sure the hinge hadn't gotten warped and that the door still shut. I knew it, and he knew it.

"You like her," he said. It was a statement, not a question.

I nodded.

"It's scary," he said, as he took a pull of the beer. He didn't mention Ashley—for which I was grateful—but she was implied.

I drank too and nodded again.

"And the worst part is that this was your mother's doing, and you don't want to give her the slightest hint that it worked."

I laughed hard then, his baritone rumble joining my laughter. It was funny because it was true.

When the laughter had run its course, we sat in silence drinking our beers. After a time, his brown eyes locked with mine and he said, "She's a good kid. Don't overthink it, go with your gut. Just call her."

I nodded, finished the beer, and we got back to work on the car.

"HELLO," SHE SAID, AFTER THE FOURTH RING.

My hands were sweating, my belly tight. "Hi..." I began, and then stopped. I was mad at myself. She was just a girl, for God's sake, get over it.

"Hello?" she said again.

"Oh... yeah... sorry. Umm. This is Nik, Nik Nichols. We met the other night at my parents' house."

I was out in the garage pacing back and forth. I had needed some privacy so had come out here after I took the requisite three days to worry like hell and then finally get my nerve up. I could feel a trickle of sweat rolling down my back and my dry mouth longing for a beer even though I had just had breakfast.

"Ummm, hmmm." She was not making this easy on me.

I took a deep breath and just got it over with. "Look. I really enjoyed meeting you. Can I take you out for dinner?" It wasn't elegant, but at least it was done.

There was silence. I am not sure how long a silence, but long enough that I felt like throwing up. I didn't know her, she didn't know me. We could be a disaster together, but there was something about her and I just had to find out what it was.

"Look, Nik, please don't take this personally," she said, and after that I was taking it real personally. "I am just not in a good place... you know?"

I licked my lips and nodded. Realizing she couldn't see me, I said, "You know what, neither am I. There has been a lot happening lately, so yeah, I get it."

"So we're good?"

"Yeah, if you go out with me we are." I winced after the words spilled out, wishing I could take them back. It was just not me. I waited helplessly for her retort, scraping my shoe on the clean cement of the garage floor.

She laughed. It was a small laugh, really only a chuckle. "Really?"

"Sorry, that came out strange, what I meant—"

"It's okay, Nik. It's okay. I appreciate your... enthusiasm."

"So, dinner? I would be happy to drive up to Flagstaff, take you wherever you want to go."

"Slow down. How about a glass of wine? I know this great winery, Page Springs Cellars, down in the Verde Valley. It's halfway between us. I have time today."

Chapter 3

Our Heroes Meet

Fall 2004, Verde Valley, Arizona

As I drove my old Ford Focus up I-17 towards Flagstaff and the Verde Valley, I replayed the conversation over and over in my head. Wondering what had worked and what hadn't. Worrying that I had made a complete ass of myself. Concerned that romantic disaster loomed large. Stunned by the suddenness of it all.

I had worked myself up to the call, that was it. When she suggested we meet today, in two hours, I was thrown way off balance. I didn't have time to plan, or prep, or... or worry too much about it. I had to change my clothes, get in the car and go.

We had tried to arrange something later in the week, but our work schedules made that difficult. So it had ended up being that same day.

I turned on the radio to distract myself. NPR was tuned in; my dad must have had it playing last time he tinkered with this car. I changed it to a classic rock station. I needed some old friends to distract me.

I wound my way out of Phoenix and started heading

up out of the Valley of the Sun. It's a steep climb up onto a rolling high-desert mesa, filled with dried grasses, a few cactus, epic views, and little else. I was nearing Cordes Junction when a blaring noise broke through Led Zeppelin's "Stairway to Heaven."

"Attention: This is the Emergency Alert System. This is not a test. Repeat, this is not a test. What is being called a sizable meteor is being tracked and headed towards Central Arizona near Camp Verde. Residents are urged to stay inside and stay off the roads. Travelers headed towards the region are urged to turn around. Repeat, a meteor is headed towards Central Arizona and expected to hit at approximately 2:00 p.m. Pacific standard time."

I glanced at the clock on my stereo. It read 1:50 p.m.

I pulled to the side of the road, emptied my pockets, throwing the contents under the driver's-side seat, got out of the car, and ran into the desert.

If anyone had been looking, I am sure I looked like a crazy man. I kind of felt like a crazy man, to tell you the truth. It wasn't something heroic and graceful. It was a hurried dumping of my pockets and a mad dash into the desert.

I saw a few other cars pulling over and people getting out. I ignored them and ran. I was looking for cover, but there wasn't much, just a few scrubs here and there. I was about to give up and risk a witness when I found a small gully and jumped in.

I let go of my biological form and summoned my neutrino form. I watched my hands turn yellow and my shirt start to smolder. I looked down at my feet. My new Simple shoes (complete with recycled tire soles, hemp uppers, and water-based glues) were smoldering too. Damn! I should have taken those off first. I had bought them right after I met her, hoping to see her again, hoping to reveal another side of myself to Licia—she lived in Flagstaff and was a rock climber, I suspected she was at least a little granola. And women pay attention to shoes, don't they?

But it was about time, and I didn't have it to spare. Licia was down there. I had no clue how I was going to stop a meteor, but I had to try.

I surrendered myself to the process, changing quicker than I had before. I leapt into the air, a yellow streak, my clothes a smoldering ruin on the ground, and headed towards the Verde Valley.

HOW DOES NEUTRINOMAN FLY? IT IS A COMMON QUESTION, one that the government spent millions trying to figure out. I suspect they thought there would be some military application if they could reverse engineer the process, but they failed.

From what I understand, from what the scientists told me, and what I have experienced over the years, it comes down to two things.

First, my body undergoes a profound shift from my biological form to my neutrino form. I am not human any-more—my neutrino form is a "coherent pattern of neutronic energy." This doesn't exactly rescind the laws of physics, but it puts me into a different category. I am governed more by quantum mechanics than Newtonian.

Second, I can control where and how that neutronic energy is released from my form. So, those yellow jets coming out of the soles of my feet and the palms of my hands power me to flight. Kind of like Iron Man, but you don't have to scratch your head wondering where all the fuel is stored. I am one big nuclear reaction.

Back then I wasn't all that refined in my skills; it took time to really get good at it. I was, though, capable of reasonably accurate flight. And boy was it fun!

I SOARED OVER THE MESA THAT SITS BETWEEN THE VALLEY of the Sun and the Verde Valley. Cordes Junction passed by in a blink, not more than a few gas stations and an artist's community. I searched the skies for the meteor and spotted some fiery streaks heading towards Camp Verde, which sat right in the middle of the Verde Valley.

The Verde Valley is a broad green valley that sits between the Mogollon Rim and Flagstaff to the north and the large mesa Cordes Junction sits on to the south. "Verde" means green in Spanish—aptly named, huh? It has one of Arizona's rare rivers, the Verde, running through it and a bunch of small towns nestled here and there.

I increased my speed as much as I could. It wasn't what I would soon be capable of (no sonic booms this time), but it wasn't bad. Then next thing I noticed were bolts of lightning flying up from the ground near the river. The lightning jumped from the ground and impacted some of the smaller rocks, exploding them into dust.

I smiled. I had, of course, been briefed on Lightningirl, but we had never met.

She was standing in the median between the northbound and southbound lanes of I-17, right in front of the bridge that crosses the Verde River. There was a smoldering wreck in the northbound lane and a large hole in the southbound lane blocking traffic. People were milling about, staring, whispering, and pointing.

I came to a rather ungraceful landing, first stumbling,

and then falling flat on my face, coming to a rest several feet in front of her. If my face hadn't been yellow, I'm sure I would have turned red. I could blame it on my poor track record with landings (and that was part of it); but mostly, I think, it was her. She stood there, a coruscating display of electrical energy in the shape of a beautiful woman. I was a bit distracted. After all, what was there not to like?

She laughed. Not a sly snicker, or a suppressed hoot, but a full-on guffaw. Her laughter was loud and sharp and carried a long distance.

I was about to say something when her laughter was replaced by an intake of breath and an "Uh oh."

I turned and looked, a clumping of about twenty bowling ball sized meteorites were headed right for us. Her lightning bolts stabbed out from both her hands, but it wasn't going to be enough.

Those meteors would kill most of the crowd.

I didn't think, I just reacted. From my prone position, I held up both hands in front of me to protect myself. A column of yellow shot out from my chest, forming a large shining yellow shield in front of us all.

The meteorites impacted the shield and evaporated with a sizzling sound, like ice on hot grill.

"Nice," Lightningirl said. It helped take out some of the sting of the laughter.

"Thanks," I replied, getting up and taking a step towards her.

When I did, small threads of electricity jumped from her body to mine, and small tendrils of neutronic energy jumped from my body to hers. The feeling was... well, it was electric, and energizing, and exciting, and not wholly comfortable.

I ignored it for a moment and turned to the crowed.

"Go! Run! Get under the bridge," I shouted, pointing to the bridge that was about fifty yards away. "I don't think we've seen the last of this."

Some people turned and started to walk, some ran, some stood there gawking at us.

Lightningirl turned then, pointing her hands towards them, her fingers splayed. "Go!" she shouted, as ten tiny bolts of electricity flashed out from her fingers and connected with the ten closest gawkers. They yelped and ran.

"Nice," I said.

"Thanks," she replied.

The energy was still flowing between us, and I was feeling... it was hard to describe it, but I felt buzzed (more buzzed than my Neutrinoman norm) and strong (stronger than my Neutrinoman norm).

I had opened my mouth to say something about it when she cut me off. "Oh my God," Lightningirl said as I turned from the fleeing bystanders and looked south.

Up in the sky, barreling down upon us, was the flaming, spitting meteor the emergency alert had been about. It was huge, a football field across, and about ten seconds from making landfall right on top of us.

This thing was moving faster, much faster, than the speed of sound. Its trajectory was all the more terrifying because of the eerie silence.

Chapter 4

Ashley

Nik's Past 1995–1998

I'M AFRAID THAT I'M TERRIBLY NEW TO THIS MEMOIR THING. How should it all go together to make any kind of sense? How do you give enough history without being boring? Which pieces add to the story and which others take away?

And I guess to understand me in 2004, you have to know just a bit about my past. One person really.

Ashley Long.

A tall, curvy, athletic blond with almond-shaped green eyes. The kind of girl that never bought herself a drink at a bar. The kind of girl that could get herself out of a traffic ticket with a flirty smile. The kind of girl that never goes for an average guy like me.

Ashley Long. I've mentioned her but really have been avoiding the reality of her in telling this story. As much as I want to, I can't. You won't understand my romantically bumbling thirty-year-old self without knowing about her, about us. So here goes.

I met her on May 5, 1995, in my ECON 301 course. I was a twenty-year-old junior at Arizona State University

(ASU—go Sun Devils!) studying business. Ashley was in the same class. I had noticed her—every male and most of the females had noticed her. She had this authoritative walk, like she always knew what she was doing. She was beautiful, tall, and had an unerring sense of fashion. As the saying goes: girls wanted to be her, boys wanted to be with her.

I had said hello to her a few times, prompted by my buddy Robby Holmes. Rob wasn't in the class, but after hearing me wax all poetic about her, he had shamed me into action. But nothing happened when I did speak to her. Just a tight-lipped smile and a nod and then back to her fashionable friends that she sat with.

Anyway, during the class final—glorious multiple choice—I caught her taking a look at my test. I was a solid B student. Not the best, but I did okay. I kept catching motion in the row behind me and smelling whiffs of her flowery perfume (smelled kind of like lilacs to me). We were seated in one of those big classrooms with raised seating, each row back higher than the last. I turned and caught her eye as she craned forward. She flushed—I had never seen her embarrassed before—and leaned right back. I moved my test so she could see it easily. What the hell. It was her education, not mine.

After class she lingered, so I did too. We were both standing, about to leave, when I said, "Maybe you should buy me a coffee now."

"What?" she asked, her furrowed brow marring her normally smooth forehead.

"I don't mind being used," I said, a silly grin on my face. "I just prefer a little foreplay first." Cocky, right? Well, I was a bit different back then, and I figured if I didn't do something Rob would never let me hear the end of it.

Her eyes narrowed and she looked me up and down like I was some piece of meat, her green eyes settling on my brown. I felt my cheeks flush and was about to turn to go when she said, "No. Sorry." She paused, our eyes still locked, before a smile broke out on her face. "Coffee's not enough. I'll buy you dinner instead."

FORTUNE FAVORS THE BOLD—WELL, AT LEAST SOMETIMES. Ashley and I had a great time at dinner that night. She was smart and funny and more than a little full of herself. But from my point of view—a twenty-year-old male looking at her—she deserved to be a bit full of herself. I insisted on returning the favor and buying her dinner the next night. I knew I was way out of her league, but the semester was winding up and I was feeling daring, hoping for a fun summer.

She accepted and one thing led to another and six months later we were living together in a crappy little apartment south of the university. I was stunned, really. Ashley Long and Nik Nichols. No one would have predicted it.

I had hit her at just the right time. She was tired of the beautiful rich boys using her and leaving her. She was in the mood for a nice guy. And she said she liked my eyes. Said they were soulful.

If I had to pick a few words to describe Ashley (beyond the physical) I would say: stubborn, athletic, and mercurial.

It's the last one that bears the most attention in this story. She was the very definition of mercurial. Her moods would change as fast as the stock market. She was intensely focused and driven as long as she was interested in something, but that could change at any moment.

I learned all about this our first winter together when she wanted to go up to Flagstaff and ski. She had never skied before and by the end of the day was better than I was. I was no champ, but I had done it a few times a year since I was a teenager. I thought I would be teaching her something, but her focus, drive, fearless attitude, and athleticism came together and she was a wonder to watch.

That season she got better and better and better. She would carve up the slopes with an eerie grace, her long blond hair flowing behind her, her body clad in only the best Patagonia coats and hats.

I told her she should get serious, that she could probably go pro. She agreed and dove in with gusto. Reading, learning from the best she could find, taking trips with me to Colorado and Utah for better snow. And then...

And then she was just done. Two seasons of skiing and she was bored. One day she was on track to go pro, the next day she had everything up for sale on eBay and was done.

I was stunned. I couldn't believe it.

I BET YOU KNOW WHAT'S COMING. ROBBY DID. MY PARENTS did. All my friends did. But me? Totally clueless. They tried to whisper it to me, saying she was changeable, "like the wind." But I was just a fool in love and told them that's what made her so great.

Ashley and I were a couple for exactly three years and five days. In May of 1998, she was done with me. Just like her skiing adventure. One day we were in love and she couldn't be happier. I had been shopping for diamonds, trying to figure out when to pop the question. And the next day she had gone all mercurial and was moving out.

"Why, Ash?" I asked her. We had both graduated and were living in a slightly less crappy apartment. I was working as a manager for a car wash (kinda using my business degree, but hoping to move up to corporate soon) and she had been through six different jobs since school, the last one as a graphics designer building websites.

She shrugged and kept stuffing clothes (not folding mind you) into her Neiman Marcus luggage.

"Is there someone else?" I asked, feeling like I stood on a high precipice, my stomach falling out of my body, sweat stinging my back, my nose full of her lilac scent.

She snorted and gave me a twisted grin that said, *Are you nuts? You know me. My reasons aren't like other people's. I am not one of the common people.*

I begged. I pleaded. I cried. She left.

To this day I can't stand the scent of lilacs.

IT'S FUNNY (AS IN IRONIC) BUT I USED TO CALL HER "ASH." No one, surprisingly, had ever done that. She thought it was cute. She liked it. After the tides changed and she left me, I felt like she had left me as a little pile of ash. The Nik that existed before then—not totally together but happy and having a general idea of where he wanted to go—was gone. All that was left was the desiccated remains of my emotional self. (And yes, I am being dramatic here. I was young. I had just lost what I thought was the love of my life. I was feeling very dramatic.)

I quit my job at the car wash, took a year off to "hike" through Europe—I spent most of my time in pubs—and then just drifted. I took uninspired jobs, had uninspired relationships, and just let the years fly past.

Earlier in this story, I wasn't honest. I wasn't telling the truth about why I was drifting. Why I was thirty and unattached. Why I had really settled for a janitor's job at Palo Verde. It wasn't as if I was still grieving the loss of Ashley (I wasn't that lame). It was just that her departure took away my momentum at a crucial time and I hadn't gotten it back.

And here's what's really ironic (as in funny): without Ashley and her abrupt taking-the-wind-out-of-my-sails departure, none of this would have happened. Neutrinoman, the war turning out like it did, Licia, me and Toxicwasteman. None of it.

Because of her I eventually became a janitor. Then I became Neutrinoman. Then I met Licia. Then things changed, boy did they change.

Chapter 5

Meteorite in Sight
Fall 2004, Verde Valley, Arizona

I'D LIKE TO SAY THAT MY SUBSEQUENT ACTIONS IN REGARDS to the flaming demon of a meteor were taken with confidence and awareness. But, alas, I cannot. They were done with fear and trepidation, and a complete lack of confidence in the result. I am told, however, that it doesn't matter, and that I looked very confident.

I was pretty sure Lightningirl and I could survive this. We could both get out of the way quick enough: me flying and her going fully electrical. But I feared for the entirety of the Verde Valley. A meteor that big could do a lot of damage. West of Flagstaff is Meteor Crater. It's about 4,000 feet across and 600 feet deep and was caused by a meteor that was only about 150 feet in diameter, nothing like this monster.

I leapt skyward, jets of neutronic energy thrusting me forth. I flew on instinct, faster and surer than I had before.

I also loosened the control on my neutronic reaction—kind of like they do in the reactor: I, metaphorically, raised the control rods all the way up, and at the same time strengthened my containment of the energy.

I am told that I became brighter and brighter until my light rivaled that of the sun.

I didn't put up a shield, or shoot neutron bolts, I just let my reaction grow stronger, my body grow hotter. I ran straight into the meteor, gave it a heartbeat (not that I had a heart at the time) and completely let go of containment.

I knew there might be some radioactive consequences to this, but it was better than total oblivion for those below.

I could feel the rock melting around me. I heard an explosion. I saw that I was falling, but couldn't do anything about it, my resources were spent. I noticed bolts of lightning jabbing up and striking all around me.

When one of the bolts impacted me, I felt myself come back to life, just a little bit. As I fell, with the remainder of the meteor all around me, I stabbed out again and again with neutrino bolts, reducing more of the rock to vapor.

"ARE YOU OKAY?" LIGHTNINGIRL ASKED, LOOKING DOWN at me as I lay in the small, smoking crater I had made in I-17 when I landed.

"Zzzz," I began. I was desperately short of energy, close to turning back to flesh—which would be quite inconvenient—and dazed from the expenditure of energy and force of my landing.

She moved to the edge of the crater and squatted down looking at me. Her left hand was extended out, with electricity arcing to it—she was drawing energy from the power lines that ran along the highway. As she drew closer, sparks flew from her to me, giving me a sip of energy and clearing my head.

"Zap me," I said, clearly this time.

She stared for a moment, her scintillating electric head forming a smile, her shoulders shrugging. "Okay. You asked for it."

She extended her right hand towards me and lightning arced from her to me. It was potent, and uncomfortable, and exactly what I needed.

When I felt myself come back (or rather when I couldn't stand it anymore), I rose, held my palm up and shouted, "Enough."

She relented, stepping back far enough so our spontaneous energy exchange ended too. She stood higher than me (I was still in the crater), her left hand still drawing energy from the power lines.

"Thank you," I said. I looked around at the destruction. The area was pockmarked from the small meteorite impacts; there were some small fires burning, I heard sirens, and saw a few people coming out from under the bridge. "So, how'd we do?"

She smiled, "Not bad."

Her smile seemed familiar. With a start I remembered where I was going before all this began: Licia and the winery.

"So, ahh," I began. "Nice meeting you. I gotta fly."

With that I leapt in the air and flew back towards my car.

I DIDN'T HAVE MUCH TIME, I KNEW IT. THAT JUMP START Lightningirl had given me wasn't going to last long. I aimed myself directly at my destination and got as much momentum going as possible.

And good thing too. Once I was halfway there, I felt the neutrino jets coming out of my feet begin to falter and I had to take them down to a minimal level. I used my momentum and began a somewhat controlled descent back towards my car.

When I was about three hundred yards away and one hundred feet in the air, the jets cut out completely and I fell. I managed to hold onto my neutrino form long enough that my impact into the ground was nothing more than jarring.

I crawled out of the little crater naked and made my way back to the car. I ran low and fast, trying to cover my private parts and keep an eye on the highway. It was, thankfully, devoid of traffic, and I made it to the car without being seen.

First, I run away from the car like a madman, and then a little while later I sneak back without any clothing on. See why I was glad there were no witnesses?

I was starving and dehydrated. My neutrino form uses everything in me it can for fuel: food, water, even my waste products. Depending on how much energy I expend, it can consume some or all of it. This time was all, and my physical condition was not good.

I crawled into the backseat, grabbed the gallon jug of water I keep back there and a granola bar and started to refuel. Once something was in my belly, I put on the spare set of clothing I had stashed and got into the front seat bringing the water with me.

I felt ill and exhausted, but I was somewhat functional.

I fished the rest of my stuff out from under the front seat. When I pulled my phone out I saw I had two text messages.

The first text message was from Palo Verde: "Your presence is required ASAP. Urgent."

The second was from Licia: "I'm okay, I hope you are too. Given the meteor incident, we will have to reschedule."

I laughed, the "meteor incident" was an interesting way to describe it. Understated and factual. I was even more intrigued.

.

Chapter 6

My Kingdom for a Costume
Fall 2004, I-17, Central Arizona

YOU KNOW HOW IN ALL THE COMIC BOOKS AND SUPERHERO movies that somehow our superheroes, despite their devastating superpowers, always have some convenient high-tech material that they can use as a costume? How no matter the force or the gyrations our superhero goes through, the costume somehow survives without a scratch. Shoot Superman and you discover that not only is he the man of steel, but those bullets don't even do a thing to his blue tights.

Well, that's just not the way it is. I have asked, whined, begged, and pleaded to no avail. It just isn't possible. The force of my neutrino radiation and emissions is just too powerful. So I have to live with it (or rather, without it).

I have to strip before each change, or watch my clothes turn to ash, and deal with it on a janitor's salary. That's right folks, Neutrinoman used to shop for clothes at Goodwill and Wal-Mart. And I have to come out of a change naked and often in the most embarrassing places.

Because of this I started drinking less beer and working

out more. My neutrino form looks like me, and well, if I am going to be parading around naked (even as a scintillating yellow nuclear reaction), I want to look good.

So why, you might be asking yourself, am I rambling on about costumes and clothes when the largest meteor in the last 50,000 years almost decimated part of my home state?

Well, it is simple really: the same is true of Lightningirl. Her lightning body will burn clothes off just as easily as my neutrino body.

Which means the curves I saw as we fought together were her curves.

And they were nice.

And I'm a man, so I do tend to notice these kinds of things.

Besides, my classic rock radio station had been interrupted by news coverage of the event, and they kept mentioning us, but boy did they get a lot wrong.

They reported my actions pretty accurately but not Lightningirl's. Eyewitnesses reported that she attacked the crowd with lightning (which she did, just to get them out of danger, and she didn't hurt anyone), and that she attacked and chased off Neutrinoman after he had saved the day (she had saved me from exposure of both my secret identity as well as my lily-white flesh).

The news was obsessed with it. "What is wrong with Lightningirl, has she changed sides?"; "Has Neutrinoman met his match?"; "Neutrinoman Saves, Lightningirl Lashes Out."

I shook my head chuckling. She must be pissed.

MAYBE I SHOULD BACK UP A BIT.

There is a lot of inaccurate information about what happened to us when the cosmic rays hit and the accidents happened. And that is to be understood; there just isn't a lot we really know.

So here is what we do know.

All three factors (accident, cosmic rays, and animal bite) combined to make us the morphs we are today. The same basic formula happened to the twenty-one superheroes and supervillains created that day, although the last factor is variable (not everyone was bit). For example: Toxicwasteman was created during a chemical spill at the Hillington chemical plant in Tucson. He wasn't bitten; he smoked genetically modified tobacco, and that was his third element.

In all cases, that third piece is taking something external into your system proximal to the event.

Okay, so that is the general creation formula.

The results actually vary quite a bit. Lightningirl and I are what are classified as quantum-metamorphs. Meaning we change at a quantum level into a different form when we manifest our superpowers. We are literally not biological, not human, when it happens. Our consciousness is there, our memories (usually), but not our bodies. I am a nuclear reaction, she is an electrical reaction.

The others morphed on a quantum level, but only once and permanently. They are referred to as quantum-biomorphs. In other words, they always have their powers, are biological, and usually don't change form. For example, Dr. Cheese always has his enzymatic superpowers ready to wreak havoc.

Whether quantum-metamorphs or quantum-biomorphs, we are all quantum-morphs and are called, for short, q-morphs.

I LISTENED TO THE NEWS THE WHOLE WAY BACK. THEY didn't know any more than I did. I wanted to know how the meteor ended up smashing into us with so little warning; don't we track near-Earth asteroids?

How can something like this just happen?

I would like to say that my mind stayed sharply focused on the problem at hand, but it didn't. It kept wandering back to, what I perceived as, the two intriguing women in my life: Lightningirl and Licia.

It sounds trite, right? A catastrophe was just averted and I was thinking about girls. Well, a woman... she was no girl.

My mind bounced back and forth between the two topics all the way down to Palo Verde.

When I got to the guard's station, they waved me through and there was a golf cart waiting for me.

I got in, and the driver, an army corporal, whisked me past two sets of cooling towers and into a squat brick building not far from reactor number three.

This was Neutrinoman headquarters. I am not sure what it used to be, but after the accident the building was taken over by the military and it is where I spent most of my time when I was here.

There was more security here—I actually had to show my badge—and I was hurried into the situation room. It's a large area on one end of the building with monitors and a few whiteboards on the walls, lots of people milling about, and a big table in the middle.

There was the usual assemblage of scientists and military. What was surprising was seeing Colonel Williams saluting and taking orders from someone else. Usually he was in charge of the place.

The army general being saluted was a big man with snow-white hair and three stars resting on each shoulder. Williams waved me over and introduced us. "General Markus, this is Nik Nichols."

I took his proffered hand and shook it. His hands were big and he had a firm grip. "We have a hell of an issue here, son," the general said. "That meteor that you stopped was a baby compared to what is coming."

I opened my mouth to speak but was distracted by one of the large LCDs on the wall. It had a graphic showing the Earth and a large object heading towards it. Below it was a countdown timer: 72 hours, 34 minutes, 10 seconds.

The general followed my gaze to the LCD monitor and said, "It's a planet killer, son. Now let's get down to business. We need to know everything about your encounter with this monster's little brother. Everything."

So I told him, not that there was much to tell. I heard about the meteor coming in, changed, and with Lightningirl's help, fought the thing.

He was particularly interested in how I destroyed the large meteor.

"So you exploded it from the inside?" the general asked.

"Yes sir. But, I don't think I can do that for this one. It is—what?—several thousand times the mass?"

The general nodded. "Sorry to tell you this, son, but you are the best chance we've got."

"What? No space shuttle standing by with a crew of scrappy oil rig workers?" I asked with an ironic smile on my face.

The general looked puzzled. "Excuse me, son?"

"*Armageddon*... You know, the movie? Came out a few years ago. Bruce Willis. Big asteroid headed for the earth..."

His mouth set, he stared at me and then shook his head. "Can you tell me anything else? Anything at all?"

"Well," I began, "after I landed, rather ungracefully, I had Lightningirl zap me. I was out of energy, and she gave me enough to get me back to my car before I was completely out."

The general's green eyes got big. "Williams!" he yelled. "Williams! Get Lightningirl in here. Now!"

My heart leapt into my mouth. She was coming. She was coming here.

Chapter 7

Into the Void

Fall 2004, Palo Verde Nuclear Generating Station, Arizona

So, can Neutrinoman survive in the void of space? That was the question the scientists went about determining, as I was shuffled to and fro trying to keep focused on the task at hand, but being distracted by one thing: Lightningirl. I was going to meet her. I was going to know who she really was.

I was excited, but frankly feeling a little guilty. Licia... what about her? Superhero she may not be, but she was a hell of a woman. And our first date was preempted by that damn meteor. I wanted to call her, double-check that she was okay, but Jennifer Johnson, one of the scientists there, was guiding me to reactor number three.

Reactor number three is mine. Well, it does provide power to the area, but it is *mine*. It has been adjusted for the use of Neutrinoman.

"God, you look awful, Nik," Jennifer said as she walked with me down the long corridor. Jennifer Johnson looked like one of those nerdy types in the comic books. You know the ones. Nerd glasses, hair up, nasally voice, loose-fitting clothing. The one the hero never notices, until one day she lets down her hair, takes off her glasses, and boom... she's a world-class babe.

She looked like that. She's African American with intelligent brown eyes, curly jet black hair pulled up in the back, and full lips.

I know what you're thinking, believe me, the thought had occurred to me. Jennifer is kind and beautiful, knows who I am, and is about my age. I should ask her out. But she is married to Jack Johnson, another scientist on the project, and probably the nicest person you could ever meet. They weren't the top scientists there, but they were my favorites. I worked with them all the time and we spent free time together too. You know, pool, barbecue, the zoo— just normal stuff.

"Nik," Jennifer said, my head was still lost in Lightningirl land and I hadn't answered her. "I said you look awful. That run at the meteor really took it out of you."

I nodded. "Yeah, everything I had. But, the tank wasn't full."

"Well then, time to fill up. And be quick with it. They've almost got the vacuum chamber ready."

I went through the door. It was like one of those you see in a submarine; round wheel that opens and closes it, seals it up tight.

Beyond the door was my dressing room. No sense burning through my clothing. I quickly undressed and went through another submarine door, down a short hallway, yet another sealed door, and into the containment chamber.

As I got closer I could start to feel it. It is hard to describe, but it is a bit like going out on a warm sunny day after a long, long winter. I could feel this warmth and energy just creeping into me. I sighed and relaxed.

The containment chamber is a large cement cylinder with a round top and walls six feet thick. Palo Verde is a pressurized water reactor; the inside of the chamber contains a series of tall metal vessels that house the reactor in the center, surrounded by the steam generators, and tubing that moves the water and steam. It's hot and noisy inside and fairly crowded. I always feel like I'm in some kind of fifties-style science fiction movie in that big space with all the glistening metal and odd noises.

The reactor stands out because of the bristling metal poles on top. These house the control rods that can be moved into the reactor to slow down the reaction. They are great at absorbing neutrinos, just like me.

I threaded my way through the maze of equipment, over close to the reactor, and sat down on a small cement bench that they had put in there for me.

I didn't change into my neutrino form; there was no need for it. I just sat there like an old man in a sauna soaking up the juice. It didn't take long, maybe twenty minutes. They had the thing cranked up.

After I got dressed and left my dressing room, Jennifer was there. She patted my face and said, "Now that's better, got some color in your cheeks now."

Jennifer led me back through the underground tunnel to headquarters and right out a side door.

Sitting there on the back of a flatbed was a large decompression chamber. It looked like you could fit twenty people in there. I wondered where the hell they had gotten this from, and so quickly. We are landlocked in Arizona, after all.

But you know the military. End of the world and all. If

they couldn't come up with a space shuttle and Bruce Willis, at least they could come up with this.

Interlude 1

So Boring

Spring 2025, Casita de Soledad, Central Arizona

I LOOKED UP FROM MY WRITING WHEN I HEARD LICIA CLEAR her throat. She was reading over my shoulder from across the room. We had a little desk set up in our living room. It was nighttime and she had been on the couch reading. She had damn good eyesight. I think it is one of the raven-like qualities she acquired during her accident.

I pushed back and swiveled in my chair to face her. "Yes, dear?" I asked.

"Bor-ring," she said in a singsong tone with an impish frown on her face.

"What?"

"Boring. So they stuck you in the chamber, you went neutrino, they sucked the air out, you were a bit freaked, but in the end they discovered you could survive in a vacuum. Bor-ring."

"Well..." I began defensively. "It was scary as hell. I was used to breathing in my neutrino form. It wasn't easy learning how not to. It was quite a challenge."

"Boring."

"And I almost melted the thing down around me during my initial *reaction*."

"Reaction? You mean world-class freak-out, don't you?" She frowned as she stared down at me.

"Hey!" I said, rising from my chair and folding my arms in front of me. Her frown turned into a grin, and I knew she had just been messing with me. "So you really think it is boring?"

"I do. Skip ahead to the part where you meet me. Now that's exciting. Man and woman, the human heart, everyone can relate to that."

Chapter 8

Missile Attack

Fall 2004, Palo Verde Nuclear Generating Station, Arizona

WHEN I WALKED BACK INTO THE COMMAND CENTER AFTER the vacuum testing, I noticed a new presence. I could only see the back of her, but she had long black hair, perfect posture, and was standing talking to General Markus. It had to be her. It had to be Lightningirl.

I walked over, my mouth dry, my palms sweating. The general noticed me and waved me over. "There you are, Nik. It is high time you two met. Nik Nichols, this is Licia Lopez. Neutrinoman meet Lightningirl."

She turned before the general said her name, and my jaw almost dropped to the floor. My heart raced, and I felt dizzy. My only consolation was that her mouth was agape too.

The general looked from me back to her and back to me again. "Do you two know each other?"

All I could manage was a weak nod. Licia recovered more quickly. "Yes sir. Nik was the person I was going to meet when the meteor hit." My dizziness intensified—she had told him about our date? She sounded so damn casual about it.

"Do you need to sit down, son? What did that test do to you?" He guided me to a chair and called for Jennifer.

It was embarrassing. I am sure I was red, as red as Superman's cape, but I took the chair and the water Jennifer brought.

It's like this. Imagine if Lois Lane was in love with Clark Kent *and* Superman. She loved them both and was torn by it. Now imagine that she discovered they were one in the same person. That is kind of how I felt. Except that I had no idea how Licia felt about me—at least Lois Lane knew Superman dug her. Licia and I were just in the first steps of our dance together, the early delicate phase where any little thing can ruin it.

I was exceedingly grateful when Jennifer dragged me off to the medical lab and checked me out.

"Nik..." she began as she was putting her stethoscope and blood pressure cuff away. "You have been holding out on me."

"I..." I began weakly. "It's kind of new."

"And you liked her before you knew she was Lightningirl. Way to go."

"Huh?"

"Look, a million guys are crazy about her. She's Lightningirl, for God's sake. Having feelings for her before you knew... well, it's a good start."

"So, the test didn't do this to me?"

"No," Jennifer said laughing. "It was the girl. But I'll tell the general you were just a little dehydrated. No need to worry him."

GENERAL MARKUS AND COLONEL WILLIAMS LED LICIA and I across the pavement towards a waiting helicopter. It was one of the big grey military ones with two rotors and lots of cargo space. Jennifer was with us, as well as a few other techs, loads of equipment, and quite a few military types.

As soon as Jennifer cleared me medically, we were herded out there. I tried to speak to Licia, but she gave me a curt shake of her head. Not the right time or place—obviously—but that did nothing to quell the rioting butterflies in my stomach.

When we got to the helicopter, Licia hung back and did not climb in. "Is there a problem, Ms. Lopez?" the general asked.

"Yes sir. I don't mix well with sensitive electronics. Double that for flying sensitive electronics."

The general looked puzzled. "I thought you had that under control. The updates I have been receiving said that you have mastered that particular problem."

"Yes sir, I have sir, but not perfectly. I just don't think it's worth the risk, and..."

"And what?"

Licia's cheeks reddened as she added, "...and I don't like to fly. Just tell me where we are going, and I will meet you there."

The general was still for a moment except for his right hand rubbing his clean-shaven chin. He signaled to a lieutenant who had a tablet computer. "Show her," he grunted.

As the lieutenant showed Licia a map and then the satellite view she requested, her eyebrows raised and a small smile snuck onto her face. "Have someone meet me by these power lines. And please have them bring a robe."

Licia waved as we took off. My thoughts were not on the meteor hurtling towards our planet or the secret destination the helicopter was headed to or the training we were about to embark on. My mind was seething in jealousy at whoever was going to be there to hand Licia her robe.

My mind was somewhat eased when I heard Colonel Williams calling in the order. He insisted that it be a female officer that greeted her.

Perhaps I should take a moment to explain how Lightningirl travels. In her pure electrical form, she can ride along high-tension power lines. So, to get to her destination, she was going to zap herself along the power grid.

My mind was wandering, ping-ponging between meteors and women. Well, *a* woman and *a* meteor. In both cases I had far too little information to go on. I didn't know much more about the meteor other than it was going to hit us, and I hadn't had a chance to talk to Licia. So... ping—meteor—pong—Lightningirl.

The helicopter had lifted off from Palo Verde and headed northeast, skirting the little Buckeye airport and taking us towards Luke Air Force Base in Glendale, which is on the western edge of Phoenix. We were flying over Litchfield Park (a small city in the Phoenix metro area) when my ping-ponging was disturbed by the sound of a pulsing alarm and the copilot saying, "I detect weapons lock. Looks like a missile, coming in fast."

"Beginning evasive maneuvers," the pilot said.

I am a bit embarrassed to admit it, but I was grateful for the interruption to my mental loop. I looked at Colonel Williams and he gave me a sharp nod and said to one of the soldiers, "Let him out."

I ripped off my headset, dumped the contents of my pockets into Colonel Williams's lap, and stepped out of the helicopter.

I should have really looked to General Markus, he was the ranking officer, but Williams was usually the one giving me orders. Besides, I am a civilian.

As I fell, I changed into my neutrino form, losing another perfectly good set of clothes, their fiery remnants falling on the city below. I looked for and spotted the missile and the contrail it left. It appeared to have been launched from the north in the Sun City area.

I headed towards it at my best speed and weighed my options. We were over a densely populated area, which really limited what was safely doable.

As I neared the missile, its long, sleek shape not much more than a blur, I pulled up and headed straight towards the heavens. Looking behind me, I could see that the missile was following—it must be a heat seeker.

I matched speed, keeping it about fifty yards behind me and headed due west, the quickest way out of the metropolis. I also continued to gain elevation—I wanted to try my new oxygen-free mode.

The missile continued its pursuit until the Phoenix area was spread out below me, the rough rectangle of civilization sprawling across the desert with tongues of green agriculture licking out to the east and far to the west.

I managed the transition gracefully this time. I wasn't breathing and I wasn't freaking out.

I was distracted by my success and almost missed the missile running out of fuel. Fortunately my peripheral vision caught the change in motion, and I stopped admiring the landscape and saw the missile tumbling back towards the Earth.

I followed it down, keeping pace, until we were maybe 10,000 feet in elevation. I could see that we had cleared the city and the missile would come down in some small mountains west of the metro area.

I modulated my arm, bringing it to this hybrid state. Not quite human, but not radioactive enough to melt the metal.

The ground was rushing up; I was having trouble matching my speed exactly to the falling, tumbling missile. At the last moment I managed to grab the now docile missile, pulled up and flew it back to Palo Verde.

Chapter 9

Welcome to Area 51

Fall 2004, Palo Verde Nuclear Generating Station, Arizona and Area 51, Nevada

I GUESS I WAS HOPING FOR A BETTER WELCOME WHEN I got back to Palo Verde. I mean, I had saved the helicopter and everyone on board without any collateral damage, and I had brought back important evidence regarding the attack.

But I guess I get it—bringing live explosives to a nuclear power plant is not the best thing. But hey, it's not like I walked in the door with it. I landed between the cooling ponds northeast of the reactors and waved the missile back and forth, waiting for someone to notice.

The sun had just gone down and it was getting dark, so maybe that is why it took so long, but I don't know.

As I waited, and as the bomb squad was called, and as the helicopter came back, I had some time to think. And no, I didn't think about Licia/Lightningirl. I thought about the attack.

It was a hell of a risk launching a surface-to-air missile from the middle of Sun City. Whoever did it must have wanted to bring that helicopter down bad. And that meant they must have suspected what it was about. And that meant...

Well, what exactly did it mean? It was puzzling. It hinted towards conspiracy and that just didn't make sense. Who would want to stop those trying to save the world?

Like I said, I hadn't been briefed yet.

THE MILITARY BEING THE MILITARY, THINGS DIDN'T REALLY happen in what I thought would be a logical order.

What would have been logical, to me, was finding out what the hell was going on. But, that was above my pay grade. And considering the fact that I was still being paid as a janitor, everything was above my pay grade.

After the bomb squad relieved me of the missile, I let the neutrino-me go and ended up standing in the middle of the desert naked. No one had been sent out with a robe for me. No one worried about my dignity. I ended up walking quite a ways, doing my best to cover myself with my hands, until a jeep came and took me back to the headquarters building. It wasn't until I got there that Jennifer handed me a robe with an apology.

Next, off to reactor number three to recharge, then back into the helicopter—still only dressed in a robe.

I was in a foul mood, sulking in my robe as we took off and headed towards Luke again. This time we were escorted by two Apache attack helicopters and made it to the Air Force base without incident. From there we got into a plane and headed northwest.

It was dark when we left and I had been through a lot that day. I fell asleep only to wake when we landed and someone said, "Welcome to Area 51."

AFTER WE GOT SETTLED AT AREA 51 AND BEFORE I WENT to bed, I had a brief moment to call home.

"Mom?" I asked. I held the phone close to my head, I was having trouble hearing. "Mom? Are you trying to use the headset again? Make sure the mic is close to your mouth."

"...wondering where you are. Nik? Nik? Can you hear me?"

"I can hear you now, Mom. I am working."

"Working? But today was your day off. Today was your date-day." Her voice got high when she said "date-day," making me cringe.

"It is a work emergency, Mom."

"Oh... but how was your date, dear? Your date with that lovely Licia girl. She'll make you forget that horrible Ashley."

"Mom, didn't you hear the news?" I asked, ignoring the Ashley comment. "There was a meteor shower in the Verde Valley. I couldn't get to the winery."

"Well... I hope you rescheduled."

"Mom, I haven't had time for that. This is a work emergency. After you get off the phone, be sure to tell Dad I am in the middle of a *work emergency.*"

I seemed to finally break through her obsession with my love life (or lack thereof). "What kind of emergency?"

"Mom, you know I can't say. Just tell Dad. I may be gone a few days."

"Son, is everything all right? Are you okay?"

"I am fine, Mom. Tell Dad. I love you both. I have to go."

After the call I crawled into bed and knew nothing until a private woke me in the morning, predawn, for training.

LICIA AND I STOOD IN THE MIDDLE OF GROOM LAKE, AN oval of stark white, the salt and mineral leftovers from an ancient lake. There were techs with their equipment a safe fifty yards back and a large cable lying near Licia with electricity jumping from it to her outstretched hand.

Colonel Williams was in charge, General Markus having left us soon after we arrived on a mysterious errand. We had had our briefing, finally, and it had left me reeling.

There was lots of data, too much data, but one fact stood above the rest. The path of the meteor heading towards us had changed. It was one of the near-Earth asteroids that we tracked (its natural orbit taking it close to the Earth). Six days ago, it had suddenly, unnaturally, changed course. Someone or something had aimed it at us.

That someone wasn't human; we lacked the technology. The technology was extraterrestrial. The irony of it all, with the two of us standing in the middle of a dry lake bed in Area 51, was not lost on me.

We had fifty-six hours left before impact.

Lightningirl and I were the planet's only hope.

Like I said, it was a hell of a briefing.

"Ready?" Lightningirl asked me, her voice quiet and soft. She was in her lightning form, as I was in my neutrino form. We stood close enough that tendrils of energy were passing between us.

I nodded and gave her what I hoped was a reassuring smile. She threw a thumbs-up to Colonel Williams and stepped closer, putting her hands around my neck and stepping on my feet as I put my hands around her waist. It looked like we were about to slow dance. I wished.

The trickle of electricity arcing from the cable became a torrent.

"High-altitude launch test number one," Colonel Williams said on his bullhorn. "In three... two... one... launch!"

The closer we got, the more powerful our exchange of energy. As we held each other, the electricity arced from the cable to her hand and from her body to mine. At the same time, the yellow neutronic energy arced from my body to hers.

It was intense, and it was intimate, and we were being observed and filmed at the same time.

It was odd. It was strange.

"Ready?" I asked her, gazing down at her face, which came up to my chest.

She leaned her head up and smiled and said, "Let's do this." She was fully in her electrical form, but even so her smile was clear and dazzling.

I pulled her closer and took off. I had never flown with anyone before. Actually, I never expected to fly with anyone at all. I didn't expect to find someone who could handle the fully neutronic me.

I flew us up at a moderate pace. Too fast and I probably would have lost control; too slow would have been even worse. It was a clear day, and I watched, fascinated, as the large white oval of Groom Lake became smaller and smaller. The brown of the desert was nestled around it, a landing strip ran through it, and the small military base hung off the southwest corner.

I kept breathing so I could better gauge our altitude, and when it became difficult I stopped, hovering us some tens of thousands of feet above the Earth.

"You okay?" I asked, knowing she didn't like to fly.

She nodded, clearly nervous, gripping my neck tighter as she gazed down below us. "You sure know how to show a girl a good time." Her voice was a gasp; there wasn't much air up here.

"Okay, so I'm going to take us up farther, real slow. Soon we won't be able to breathe or talk, so tap me on the back twice if you get into trouble," I needed more practice flying with her, and she needed to see how it felt not breathing.

She nodded and I ended up taking us up to about 40,000 feet. It went well. On the way down, I stopped when we were still a ways up, and the air was cold but breathable.

"Can we talk?" I asked. The energy was still coursing between us, distracting me, but I had to take my chances where I could find them.

"You know they're filming us," she said, looking down at the ground below us, "they probably can hear."

"Oh..." I really did want to talk to her, hovering above the Earth was... well, it was kind of romantic.

"We'll talk later," she said, "after they are done with us. I promise."

I nodded my head and flew us back down to the ground.

WE WERE ALL TIRED. WE HAD STARTED TRAINING AT SUNUP and it was nearing 10:00 p.m. We huddled around a long conference room table taking stabs at our food and making attempts at conversation.

The room was the "war room" for us here at Area 51. On the wall was a large flat-panel display that showed the path of the meteor and the time to impact: 42h 22m 15s.

Colonel Williams looked at us, assessing our condition. Williams is a compact, athletic man with an angular face and a salt-and-pepper brush cut. He said, "I'm calling it, people. Everyone get some rest; we will resume at 0600."

Jennifer, some techs, and a bunch of military personnel

got up and shuffled out of the room. Colonel Williams still sat, transfixed by the ticking down "time to impact" display.

"Colonel?" Licia asked.

Williams looked up, his face locked in a deep frown. "Hmm?"

"Do you think General Markus can really ensure thunder clouds for us?"

He grunted a yes, his eyes not moving from the display.

"How is he going to do that?"

Williams's eyes reluctantly moved from the display to Licia. "Above my clearance, but if he says he can do it, he can do it." He slowly pushed himself to a standing position, turned, and left the room.

Licia and I sat there in silence. There were things I wanted to say, things I wanted to ask, but I was just so tired. "I think there is another one of us," I finally said.

"What?"

"Another one of us, that got caught by the cosmic radiation. We know there are more." She still looked puzzled. I was tired. I wasn't making much sense. I swallowed and tried again. "They are going to use someone like us to control the weather. It's fall, thunderstorms are rare. That is why General Markus is so sure."

Licia nodded. "I bet you are right."

We were silent again for a while. It wasn't an awkward silence, just silence. I kind of liked it, and I wouldn't have interrupted it but I felt myself starting to doze off.

"I am sorry about our date," I said.

She turned, meeting my eyes and smiled weakly. "Oh... I don't know. I've learned more about you today than in a dozen first dates combined."

I nodded. "Yeah... but—"

She rose from her chair, her hand briefly lying on top of my hand as her eyes caught mine. I felt the energy course between us, all thoughts of sleep gone. "We'll get to it, Nik. First, we save the world, then we have a real date." She yawned, her hand leaving mine and rubbing her face. "Good night," she said as she left the room.

Chapter 10

A First Date
Fall 2004, Area 51, Nevada

IT HAD TAKEN SOME DOING: GETTING UP PREDAWN (NOT A big loss; I woke up very early and couldn't go back to sleep, too much on my mind); tracking down Colonel Williams and getting his permission; going to the kitchen and getting their help. But it was worth it.

I was standing by the door to Licia's room when she opened it, sleepy eyed and yawning. We were both staying in the same building which had nice, hotel-style rooms. I think they used it for visiting officers.

"Good morning," I began. "Colonel Williams has assigned you to me until 0700."

She smiled, "Really?"

"Yes," I said smiling back, "Really. If you will come with me, my lady." I extended my arm to her and she took it, a quizzical look dancing on her round face.

We walked out of the building, around a large warehouse, and out towards the stark white expanse of Groom Lake.

The sun was not quite up, and the desert was bathed in

a warm predawn glow. Out on the lake they had constructed a circle of six metal towers, about sixty feet tall.

"Where are we going?" she asked.

"Not to worry, all will soon be revealed."

It didn't take long; soon she saw it and I heard her breath catch. It was a small table, draped with a white cloth, and two chairs. Behind it was the bulk of the dry lake bed, and behind that the gentle folds of the desert rising up into small mountains.

I took her to her chair, the one that faced the mountains, disengaged from her arm, and pulled out her chair.

"What... How..." she stammered.

I smiled, the surprise on her face was reward enough for my efforts. "Nutrition, my lady. I made a good case for nutrition." I started pulling off the metal lids from the plates one at a time. "Eggs, scrambled; fruit, fresh; English muffins with jelly; and, of course, cheese—Swiss, Monterey Jack, and Muenster."

She smiled, her hands clapping three times, as she took her napkin and put it on her lap.

"May I?" I asked, referring to the food. She nodded her head, and I prepared her a plate before preparing my own plate and sitting down across from her.

As she was eating, she said, "Seriously, how did you get the colonel to go for this?"

I shrugged my shoulders and said, "I told him if there is not time for a real date then I don't think the world is worth saving. I appealed to his latent romantic sensibilities."

She stopped eating, mid-bite, her eyebrows arched. "You didn't?"

"No, actually I didn't. I used a much more logical argument."

"What?"

"Like I said, nutrition. I don't know about you, but when I go all neutrino, my body uses anything that is not the essential me as fuel for the reaction." I gestured at the eggs and the cheese, which my plate was piled high with. "I need the densest foods I can get."

"It's not like that for me," Licia said as she spread strawberry jam on her English muffin, "I draw energy from power lines, my surroundings, or storms. I am not a barely controlled nuclear reaction."

"Barely... Barely! I take offense."

She bowed her head briefly, a smile playing on her lips. "Please accept my humble apology. I meant no offense."

"Apology accepted, m'lady; your mere presence is a balm for any slight, real or imagined."

She nodded, laughing. "So if you need dense foods, where is the bacon and the sausage?"

I paused, I wasn't sure if I had calculated correctly. "Well... I saw the way you pushed the pot roast around your plate the other night. I was guessing you don't eat meat."

She nodded, her lips pursing and her head cocking slightly to the right. I know what that look means now, but I didn't know then. That look is a mixture of mild surprise and delight, resulting in a moment of appraisal or reevaluation. It was a good sign, but I didn't know that.

"Besides," I added, trying to hide how nervous that look made me feel, "I really prefer cheese."

She really noticed my plate then. It was about one-third eggs and about two-thirds cheese. "You're not kidding."

"I blame it on the rat."

"The rat?"

"Yeah, you know, cosmic rays, combined with radiation and the rat's bite made me... Neutrinoman."

"Seriously?"

"Well... I will admit to a fondness for cheese before the accident, but after... I am just crazy about it." With that I stabbed a square of cheese and popped it into my mouth.

"So..." Jennifer asked, a look of mischief in her eyes. We were sitting together awaiting another briefing.

"So?" I asked, trying to sound innocent.

"So... How was your romantic desert sunrise breakfast?" I must have blushed, because Jennifer laughed. "Oh come on, everyone knows about it. It is not like a thing like that is going to be kept secret in a place like this. So..."

I shrugged my shoulders. "It was pleasant."

"Pleasant!? Come on, dish."

"And there was cheese," I added with a smile.

"I am sure it went fine," she said, nodding her head.

"Why?"

"First," she began, holding up a finger, "there was interest before the whole superhero thing was known. Second," she added another finger, "you're Neutrinoman, for God's sake. You can get whomever you want. Third—"

"Excuse me," I interrupted. "I can get whomever I want?"

"Well yeah, provided they are available and know who you are. You're actually a nice guy, Nik." She smiled, her brown eyes dancing. I am sure I blushed deeply. "May I continue?" she asked. I nodded. "Third, that was a big, fat, romantic gesture; not many men do that these days. Conclusion: it went well."

I wanted to talk more about this, but Colonel Williams clearing his throat to start the briefing prevented that.

Interlude 2

What is Romantic?
Spring 2025, Casita de Soledad, Central Arizona

"JENNIFER GOT IT WRONG," LICIA SAID. SHE WAS READING over what I had written so far. She held a printout of it in her hand as we lounged on our deck, the rolling high desert of Arizona laid out before us as the sun set over it.

"What?" I asked.

"She got it wrong. It wasn't the big romantic gesture that really got my attention, although that was quite nice."

"What was it?" I asked.

"A small thing, really." She lowered the papers holding them to her chest as she watched the light play along the bottom of the few clouds in our view.

"What?" I was dying to know. I knew that breakfast had had an impact, but I just had to know what it was specifically. You know, in case I needed such data in the future.

"Well, you offered me your arm. So old fashioned and gentlemanly. That was a perfect start."

"And…" I knew her well enough to know there was more.

"And…" her look got faraway, the warm sunset light

making her face even more beautiful. "And you noticed that I didn't eat your mom's pot roast."

I laughed, but only briefly, until it became clear she was serious. "Really?"

She nodded, "Really. It was the nicest thing a man had ever done for me."

"To notice you didn't eat meat?"

"No… No… Not that specifically. But to notice something about me that wasn't obvious. To notice something besides my ass and breasts on first meeting me. To see beyond the physical, that many men don't ever get past, to seeing the woman."

"Oh…" I didn't know what to say.

"You proved yourself to be… to be special. You saw *me*."

Her brown eyes were moist as they took me in. I was struck nearly dumb, only able to mumble an "I love you" as I got out of my chair, knelt in front of her, and took her hand.

She placed her palm to my cheek, a few tears rolling down her face. She then smiled playfully and asked, "I'm hungry, how about some cheese?"

Chapter 11

The Earth Below
Fall 2004, Area 51, Nevada

I ALMOST FORGOT TO MENTION THIS. RIGHT AFTER THAT breakfast on Groom Lake, our first date, Licia did something that just felled me. I guess I am learning it is the little things, really, that make the biggest difference.

I was standing, waiting for Licia to get up so we could head back for our morning briefing. I didn't offer my arm, but she came up beside me and took it anyway. Her hand, warm and pulsing with electricity, wrapped itself around my arm, she leaned close and whispered quietly, as smooth as silk, "Thank you."

We walked wordlessly to our briefing like that.

And really, if I had to point to one moment where my heart was completely lost to her, that was it. That quiet simple moment of intimacy and gratitude and hope.

It sustained me through the rest of all of this.

THERE WAS ONE MORE PLEASANT SURPRISE THAT MORNING before the hard work began. After the briefing, we were taken back out onto Groom Lake, to where the six metal towers had been built overnight.

They were each about sixty feet tall and had large cables running to them. Licia grinned when she saw them; I, however, would soon grow to hate them.

The pleasant part was the partition that had been set up for us away from the circle a bit. It was our changing room. Nothing more than a thin metal frame with black cloth over it. But it was a bit of privacy for us to go all q-morph in without having to disrobe in front of the many personnel there.

I am sure it was mostly about Licia, and I was glad they did it for her, but I appreciated it too.

This was our last full day before impact, and we worked hard.

After we had both used the "changing room" and were in our q-morph forms, the procedures began. They were a combination of experimentation and practice. To see what we were capable of.

Unlike in the comics, we weren't just suddenly proficient with our powers, it took time and effort and practice, and lots of failures.

Lightningirl looked at me and asked, "Ready?"

I took a deep breath and nodded my head.

Her form quickly changed to something not at all human—more of a human-ish shaped collection of energy—and with a loud clap, she wasn't there anymore. A lightning bolt, that is it, she became a lightning bolt. I had heard, I knew what she was going to do, but seeing it was stunning. She could become pure electricity. It was awesome.

I looked up and saw her, back in a mostly humanoid form, hovering between the six towers, bolts of electricity flowing from all of them into her.

This was her first test. Hovering.

She did it numerous times with the scientists taking

tons of readings, but each time it was the same, and each time it was impressive.

Her next test was charging me. I was pretty tapped out from yesterday. We knew that she was capable of charging me, but we didn't know to what extent.

So, with her hovering amongst the towers, she started charging me as I stood in the center of the towers below. First it was a tiny, but steady, tendril of electricity. It was sharp and insistent, but somewhat pleasant. I felt myself slowly getting stronger.

The tests ramped up until the tendril went to a bolt as thick as my arm, and the electricity she was sending ripped through me with a searing pain. The noise was deafening, almost like a continuous thunderclap.

It hurt, but it worked. After about an hour of this I was up to my normal charge level. So, they had her expand the bolt so it was bigger than my leg and continued the process for another hour.

My neutrino form could handle it, it could absorb the energy, but it went from pain to agony. I understood why we were doing it, but it was difficult. It was also a strange counterpoint to my morning and my feelings about Licia. She went from being the object of my affection to my torturer.

After the second hour was over, I was bristling with energy. I paced in a small circle over the dry lake bed. My feet turning the salt into something akin to glass because I had so much energy radiating off of me. I felt aggressive and trapped, like a hungry lion in a cage. The energy coursing through me demanded action.

After Lightningirl flashed down to the ground, I looked to Colonel Williams. He, and all the personnel, were a ways back behind thick clear barriers to protect them, and their equipment, from the radiation. I had this yellow nimbus around me, and I am sure it wasn't safe for flesh and blood to be close. Colonel Williams gave the thumbs-up.

I let out a feral grunt in relief. I double-checked that Lightningirl had moved back outside of the circle of towers. I then took off.

This flight wasn't like before; my flying up until then paled in comparison. I took all that energy that was pent up in me and let it rip. I shot into the air exceeding the speed of sound several times (I didn't know this at the time. I was too caught up in it, but instruments revealed it later).

The Earth fell away from me at an alarming rate, and I just let it. I can't say that I was thinking clearly. The energy coursing through me could not be denied.

And it happened quickly. My sense of time wasn't very accurate, but I am told it was eight minutes and forty-three seconds. At the end of that I was feeling more myself, feeling more rational.

I looked around me and saw darkness and stars. I looked below and the circle of the Earth was clearly discernible. I could see the blues of the oceans, the browns of the continents, shrouded here and there by clouds. I could make out the United States and Arizona. I saw clouds gathering off the Pacific making their way towards Arizona—that storm that General Markus had promised.

And I was still moving. The sense of movement was subtle (I was a long ways away from any point of reference), but I knew I was moving. I looked down at my neutrino form; no, I wasn't thrusting. I must have broken free of the gravity well and was coasting away from the planet.

The thought looped through my head for a few moments: I have broken free of the gravity well. I was an astronaut without a spaceship. Free of the gravity well, an astronaut without a spaceship!

It was a glorious feeling. Well, it was for the precious moments that it lasted. I then wondered, *how the hell am I going to get back?* This test had called for me to go up into the mesosphere, not to break free of Mother Earth.

Now I have been Neutrinoman long enough to gauge my energy levels, to know how much I have left in me, but back then my sense of such things wasn't all that refined. And I panicked a bit. Okay, well, I panicked a lot.

Have you ever been snorkeling? Did you ever have the experience when you are swimming along, following a beautiful tropical fish in clear warm waters, when you look down and you are suddenly in deep and murky waters?

For me, being in relatively shallow waters felt perfectly safe. I could swim all day with a mask, a snorkel, and a set of fins. But when I accidently found myself in deeper waters, thirty or forty feet; when the bottom became murky and distant; when everyone else was a long ways away; that is when I got to feel the true vastness and power of the ocean.

Well, this felt like that, except several orders of magnitude more intense.

So yeah, I freaked out.

Just like those times snorkeling, I turned back home and gave it everything I had.

Like I said, I was a long ways up. Colonel Williams later told me I was about 350 miles up. So my first efforts didn't seem to yield any results, the Earth kept receding. So I applied more power, the Earth stopped moving away, but wasn't getting bigger. I applied more and more power, until the Earth started visibly moving towards me.

And I didn't aim very well. I had a general sense of where

things were; it was kind of like looking at the satellite view on Google maps, except not as clean and with the clouds and atmosphere. So, I did head roughly towards the southern part of Nevada.

After much effort, the Earth started to move towards me in a way that was pleasant, but soon that rate became alarming. I stopped thrusting, but the world kept coming at me faster and faster. I think this was mostly perception (my point of reference being closer and closer) and gravity pulling me back.

At the same time my rate of descent started to terrify me, I felt exhaustion hit me. I didn't have much neutrino time left.

As I rocketed towards the Earth, not sure of exactly where I was, Las Vegas saved me. It is the biggest thing in the area: a sprawling city nestled in the desert with Lake Mead to the east looking something like a great blue dragon with its wings outstretched, the tip of one wing pointing towards the city.

From there I was able to spot the distinct white oval of Groom Lake to the northwest. So, I adjusted my course and tried to slow my rate of descent. But I didn't have much in me. My priority was to retain my neutrino form, without which I would die on impact.

And I did slow myself, but not nearly enough. I was several thousand feet above the lake when lightning started stabbing up from below and hitting me.

I had to smile: Lightningirl. I took everything she was pumping into me and used it to slow me down.

As it was, I landed hard. No, "landed" is not the right word. I "impacted." So right at the end, when it was clear that my rate of descent was dangerous, I veered to the north several hundred yards and plowed into the salt and minerals of the dry lake bed.

I passed out, I think only briefly, and came to in the middle of a crater about ten feet deep. I was back to my human form and quite naked. I was embarrassed but alive. And, I must admit, that my embarrassment was tempered by the memory of seeing the Earth whole and round below me. That same Earth that was under attack.

Chapter 12

The Risk is Too Much
Fall 2004, Area 51, Nevada

IT WAS LIGHTNINGIRL THAT RESCUED ME OUT OF MY crater. I am sure military personnel would have gotten there eventually, after they had checked for radiation and donned the proper gear. Lightningirl, fortunately, didn't need to do any of that.

"What's a nice guy like you doing in a crater like this?" she said from the rim.

I covered myself, flushing red, and said, "Zap me... please."

"Okay, but don't say you didn't ask for it." She really let it rip, a large bolt of lightning extending from her right hand and hitting me in the chest. I was knocked back onto the side of the crater, gasping for breath. This wasn't the baby tap she had given me up in the Verde Valley; this was a huge amount of energy. I relaxed into it, as I was slowly learning to do, and the searing agony of it faded back into intense pain.

On the plus side, it didn't take long, and soon I was back in my neutrino form and had flown out of the crater and stood beside her. Her left hand was extended back to the towers and electricity was arcing from them to her from several hundred yards away. I didn't know she could draw power from that far.

"Thank you," I said.

She nodded and continued to zap me as we walked back to the circle of metal towers.

TRAINING CONTINUED FOR THE REST OF THE DAY, IN THE same vein. Licia got better at modulating the energy she was "zapping" me with so I could better absorb it. I got better at receiving that energy, and by the end of the day I could receive a full power bolt with only minor discomfort. "Charging" also sped up from an hour to about ten minutes.

I also got better at reentry; that crater was the only one I made that day. I can't say that I got comfortable out there in the void, but I did learn to tolerate it and to judge my speed better.

We also practiced "aiming" me. Space, you know, is a big place, and when I went for the meteor I needed to be headed in the right direction. So, they deployed fighter jets, and had them circling at three different altitudes (F-16 Falcons at 40,000 feet, F-22 Raptors at 65,000 feet, and SR-71 Blackbirds at 85,000 feet). At each altitude there would be two jets, and my job was to thread between them in as straight a line as I could and hold that course once I left the atmosphere behind.

This didn't prove to work all that well. It got me headed in the right direction, but if I was even a degree or two off, I might not see the meteor.

WE HAD OUR FINAL BRIEFING BEFORE THE PLANE TOOK US back to Palo Verde. We couldn't conduct the mission from Area 51; we needed all the power we could get, and I needed the radiation.

The "charging" that Lightningirl can do for me with electricity is effective, but it is not quite the same as being exposed to the radiation that changed me.

The lightning boost is a bit like a caffeine buzz. It comes on strong and can go just as quickly. I needed the real thing. I needed serious radiation.

After the briefing, the chaos still swirled around us as military personnel and scientists went about their jobs, but it was one of the rare moments that Licia and I were alone. We were sitting at the big conference table, watching the "time to impact" display. Something had been gnawing at me, bothering me. I wish there had been more time to consider my words before I said them, but there wasn't. Licia would be "zapping" back to Arizona, and once we got back to Palo Verde I would go directly into reactor number three.

"Big day tomorrow," I began. Lame.

She looked at me, her eyes focusing, one eyebrow rising. "Umm hmm," she said with a small nod of her head.

I searched my mind for a diplomatic way to say what I wanted to say but couldn't come up with it, so I just blurted it out. "I don't want you to go up tomorrow."

"What?" she asked as if she hadn't heard me.

"Tomorrow. I don't want you to go up."

Her eyes searched my face and her brow crinkled. "I don't understand. You saw the weather forecast; there is going to be a giant thunderstorm. You are going to need all that power."

I nodded, she was right. "I know. I know. It's just..."

"What, Nik? Just spit it out."

I sighed and looked down at my hands. "If you go up, and I don't come back... Well, how will you get down? You can't fly."

The look she gave me then was danger. I didn't know that look then like I do now, but it was a signal, clear as a bell, that I should course correct immediately or suffer the consequences.

"It's a thunderstorm, I'm Lightningirl," she said, her tone icy. "I'll just ride a bolt down. Besides, they scrapped the plan of me going all the way up with you; I'll just be up there with the clouds, it's not a big deal."

"You've never done that, you don't know what will happen."

"What are you saying? I am trying to understand, but it is starting to sound like you don't need me. That you can save the world on your own."

"No... No... I..." I rubbed my face. I was exhausted, tired to the bone; the last few days had taken everything I had.

"Then what?" She was standing, her fists on her hips, the danger in her eyes now evident even to a dolt like me.

"The risk is too much."

"Too much?" she asked, her voice rising, drawing looks from the people still in the room. "Too much? You fail, we *all* die. The whole planet dies. And you're telling me that the edge I might give you, however small, is not worth having? That I should sit on the sidelines like some weak woman in need of a strong man's protection so I don't get hurt?" Sparks were starting to form on her extremities, and several strands of her hair rose up with sparks dancing on the ends.

"Please. I am not saying this right. I don't want you to get hurt."

She snorted and said, "Too late." She turned on her heel and left.

Chapter 13

The Face of a Goddess
Fall 2004, Area 51 and
Palo Verde Nuclear Generating Station, Arizona

JENNIFER LAUGHED AT ME WHEN I TOLD HER WHAT HAD happened. Not a gentle chuckle, but a full-on belly laugh with tears running down her cheeks. It hurt and confused me. She must have seen the look on my face.

We were in the little infirmary at Area 51. Jennifer was examining me before we headed back to Palo Verde. I think I told her about what had happened to avoid having an uncomfortable conversation about trying to save the world and the intense pressure I was under. Mission accomplished, we had veered into a very distracting, and entirely uncomfortable, alternate topic.

"Nik, Nik, Nik," she said, shaking her head, ripping open the Velcro blood pressure cuff. The noise almost made me jump.

"What?" I asked.

"You just told someone, who is arguably the most powerful woman on the planet, that you don't need her help. That the last forty-eight hours of training and bonding wasn't necessary. That all she learned about you as a kind and sensitive man was dead wrong." She descended into another fit of laughter.

When her laughter ended and she really looked at me again, I was staring at her. I was devastated, and I am sure it showed. "I just want to keep her safe," I said, quiet as a mouse.

Jennifer nodded, her voice gentle. "I know, and she'll figure that out, but it may take some time."

"I want us to both make it through this, but..." I couldn't continue.

She looked at me, her face serious, all traces of mirth erased. "You don't think you're coming back, do you?"

And there we were, into the topic that was my biggest worry. I got laughed at for no good reason. I shook my head, looking at my hands; I couldn't meet her eyes.

"And if you aren't going to make it, you don't think she'll survive getting back to the ground."

I didn't answer, letting my silence confirm her words. The thought had been trapped in my head for the last few days—it was strange to have it loose. I was afraid it was going to damage something, like a teenager driving his own car for the first time.

I know, I know, not the most logical point of view, but Licia was becoming precious to me and instinctively I wanted to protect her, logical or not.

"You need her, Nik. You can't do this without her. She has to go up with you. If you don't take care of that thing, we all die."

THE PLANE LANDED AT LUKE AIR FORCE BASE, AND FROM there we took a helicopter back to Palo Verde Nuclear Generating Station.

Jennifer led me right to the reactor. I thanked her for her help, and she told me to get some rest. I closed the heavy metal door behind me, the resounding clang sounding final in some strange way.

I took my clothes off, put the robe on, took the cooler full of cheese they had left, and made my way into the core of the reactor. They had it cranked, I could tell. The warmth felt good, like the sun on your face after being inside too long. It cleared my mood somewhat.

There was a cot setup for me. I was to sleep in here tonight, and absorb all the radiation I could.

I didn't think there was any chance I would be able to sleep, but minutes after loading up on cheese and lying down, I was out. The last few days had been taxing, more taxing than I would have thought possible.

Palo Verde, and everything within two miles of it, was on lockdown. The official story was there had been a credible terrorist threat on the nuclear power station. It was a cover for what we were about to do. This was in the early days, us q-morphs were not publicly acknowledged yet (by the government, at least).

We were set up in a field behind the plant, right next to the metal towers that distributed the electricity. The plant was running hot, and Lightningirl would have access to every single joule of it. We would end up blacking out much of Arizona and Southern California, but it was a small price to pay.

I walked from reactor number three to the site. Everyone gave me a wide berth. I was a bright yellow. So bright, I am told, that they couldn't look at me directly. I had never been this fully "charged" before. I felt powerful and dangerous. I worried that I couldn't keep all this energy held in.

When I got to the site, I only had eyes for Lightningirl. At a safe distance were the techs and the scientists and the brass, all huddled behind their clear shielding. But in the center of it all, huge bolts of electricity arcing from the metal towers to her outstretched hands, was Lightningirl.

She was magnificent. Her entire form crackled and popped with electricity. Her hair, snapping tendrils of energy, waved behind her head forming a nimbus halo.

She was terrifying. I may have been too bright to look at, but she was too brilliant to look away from. She looked like one of the old goddesses come alive: Shakti, Medusa, Kali, Aphrodite. She looked like she could kill you with one glance.

I wanted to talk to her, I wanted to plead for forgiveness, to admit my stupidity, to bow to her beauty and power. But I didn't... thank God. There was a job to do and that was all that mattered.

Realizing that I had stopped and had been staring at her for some time, I moved over to the launch area. It was nothing more than a loose circle marked with ammo cans about ten yards from Lightningirl.

The signal was given and the goddess in front of me turned her gaze, her attention, her power to me. The bolts of lightning stabbed out from her right hand and hit me in the chest.

It was a huge amount of energy, much more than she had managed at Area 51. And, seeing the nuclear power plant behind her, it was easy to tell why. She had enough electricity to power four million homes available to her and was pumping all she could into me.

I imagined that the goddess in front of me was angry, that I had done something unforgiveable, that this was punishment. And, I probably wasn't far off.

The energy poured into me, and I did not resist. It was painful but bearable. My increased base of neutronic energy allowed me to accept much more electrical energy than I had before.

This went on for some minutes, I don't really know how long, until a flash came from the assembled brass telling us to proceed to the next phase.

She moved into the circle. I smiled, but I am not sure how clear it was to her. My form was pulsing with a bright yellow glow around it; it is possible she couldn't even see my face.

"Ready?" I asked.

She nodded once, sharply, and put her hands around my shoulders and stepped onto my feet as I put my arms around her waist.

Another flash from the brass and I took us up. I used the smallest trickle of power. Fortunately, I realized that in my overpowered state, doing this normally would get us both into orbit before we knew it.

We eased up into the sky and headed towards the leaden clouds above us. In the distance I could hear the rumble of thunder and caught the stabbing flash of lightning over the desert to the west.

When we entered the clouds, everything went dim and it was as if we were alone, as if there was no one else in the world. I was still carrying us upwards, but the sense of motion was lost to the grey. It was like we were two dancers slowly turning on some smoky dance floor.

"I'm..." I started, but found I had to swallow. "I'm so sorry."

She looked at me, her eyes those of a goddess, and smiled. It was a small smile, perhaps an indulgent smile, but a smile nonetheless.

"I just don't want you to get hurt."

She shook her head then, just as we rose above the clouds into the bright sunshine.

"I'm not exactly some wilting violet. I can take care of myself."

Tendrils of electricity were stabbing out of the clouds and arcing to her body. Her hair was a wild cloud of sparks around her. I felt her weight lift from me, and as she let go of my neck, I let go of her waist. She floated on those tendrils a foot in front of me.

"I can see that," I said.

She nodded once, like a judge banging down a gavel. The matter was settled.

"These clouds are loaded, can you handle more?"

I wasn't sure that I could, but I knew I would need it. I glanced up and saw the first set of jets circling above us, and then above them, almost out of sight, I saw the second set. I lined myself up so I was pointed in the right direction and said, "Bring it on."

"Nik," she said, her voice soft, sounding more like Licia than Lightningirl.

I looked from the planes back to her.

"Get that damn thing and come back. Okay?"

"Okay," I said nodding, and looked back up. I couldn't hold her gaze. Her face, still the face of the goddess, showed worry and fear and doubt—all the things that I was feeling. In some ways it was a relief, and in other ways it was terrifying. Just, exactly, how long a shot was this?

I heard the crackle of energy, saw the flashes of light out of my peripheral vision, and felt the bolt of lightning stab into me.

Chapter 14

Desperately Seeking Meteor
Fall 2004, Above the Earth

I GASPED, THIS WAS EVEN MORE ENERGY THAN I HAD received before, but I relaxed and let it in.

It took everything I had, but I held steady, sighting my trajectory, and staying put. I wanted to move, I wanted to shout, I wanted to explode, but I didn't. I let it in, feeling the frenetic electrical energy build on top of my neutronic energy. I felt myself expanding, my world turning a yellow hue as the yellow nimbus around me expanded larger and larger.

Just when I thought I couldn't stand it, just when I thought I would explode right there, I let the tiniest trickle of energy in the form of additional thrust out and shot forward.

I had done my best to regulate the energy, but I blew past the first set of planes, the second, and the third that I hadn't seen from above the clouds and shot into orbit.

As I passed them, my trajectory had looked good, but I kept accelerating for a long, long time, I had a very long way to go.

As the Earth receded behind me, I searched for the meteor; I couldn't find it. It was big, about a mile across, but it was a speck in the vastness of space.

I kept an eye on the Earth, and when it became the appropriate size—the size of a pie pan from ten feet away, we had practiced this—I arrested my motion and began reversing it, attempting to match the speed of the rock as it hurled towards the planet.

I was about 20,000 miles above the Earth, right about where the meteor should be. I could see the whole of the Earth—a gorgeous blue marble floating in the inky black of space. If I had been breathing, it would have taken my breath away. It was hard to believe impact was in less than one hour.

Where was the damn meteor?

I sent out the flares: two neutrino bolts, one to my left, and one to my right. This was the agreed upon symbol; it told those watching I didn't find the meteor and to signal its location.

I was tempted to begin searching, but I didn't; I waited. The problem was I could go farther off course without knowing it. What I did do was slowly rotate myself, keeping half an eye on the planet and letting my peripheral vision search for motion.

After a time... I really couldn't tell you how long. Out there time was strange; I think it was no more than about ten minutes, but it felt like it could have been days. I was anxious, still bristling with energy.

After a time, I caught a flash of light planet-ward; it was one of the missiles exploding that they had sent up with me. I sent out a single flare to let them know I had seen it and kept watching. Soon a string of three dots slowly started to resolve. These were my reinforcements. Unlike me, they had radar and telemetry and guidance. They may not be able to destroy the meteor, but they could find it.

I waited until the missiles were visible enough for me to gauge their direction and then I adjusted my course. I kept the meteor-matching earthward momentum but moved sunward. My course hadn't been off by much, but at this distance out it put me hundreds of miles away.

The size of the thing took my metaphorical breath away, once I could see it. It was made of dark rock and would have been hard to see even if I had been right on top of it. I maneuvered so that the sun was behind it, backlighting it with a yellow halo.

It was vaguely ovoid and gently rotating.

I stared. A mile across and I had to vaporize the thing. Doubt, sharp and visceral, found me. How the hell could I do this?

There was a plan. It had been drilled into me, but seeing it there, I froze.

As I watched, it moved perceptibly closer to the Earth. I was more behind it now, instead of to its side. I moved around to the other side so I could get a better look.

I can't say why I did that, except I was still in shock from the size of the brute, and I was really stalling for time.

The rock was a flat grey with a smooth, gently undulating surface pitted with craters. And I saw something else: a glint of something reflective, as I passed from the shadow-side of the meteor to the sun-side. It looked metallic and large, but that didn't make any sense.

I made for it. The plan called for me to make a landing on the surface of the meteor, but that is not why I did it. It was impulse, instinct; the incongruity required investigation.

The meteor was the shape of a squat potato, with its long end headed towards Earth. The glints that caught my eye were on the back end of the rock.

As I flew in I could see more and more details. First were the large cones sticking out of the rock, with their flared, open ends, about twenty feet in diameter, pointed space-ward. There were six of these. The outside of them were a dull grey that closely matched the color and texture of the meteor. The inside of them were what glinted in the light; they were a silvery, reflective color.

Under the cones was a large bulbous sphere that at any distance would have looked like part of the meteor, but up close you could see the texture was different. It too matched the color of the meteor and had irregular lumps and bumps on it. Out of it, facing around the circumference, were several smaller cones and below those, jabbing into the rock, was a series of what looked like legs attaching it to the meteor. It was clearly man-made.

Man-made!

I floated there above it (there was no gravity of note from this thing) agape. A man-made structure. But it couldn't be a man-made structure. We had never gotten out beyond the moon. We couldn't have done this, and why would we have?

A non-man-made structure! Which meant it was... Well, if man didn't make it, then some kind of extra-terrestrial intelligence did. It was alien-made.

General Markus had not explained what had pushed this meteor out of its safe orbit and headed it towards us. He had said he didn't know and "wouldn't participate in idle conjecture."

Well, it wasn't idle conjecture anymore. This meteor had been weaponized and pointed right at us.

Interlude 3

Casita de Soledad
Spring 2025, Casita de Soledad, Central Arizona

"Meteor? Why do you keep calling it a meteor?" Licia asked. She had been reading over my shoulder again as I wrote.

"Well," I began, "it is a meteor." She shook her head. "What is it then?" I asked. "It's not a big snowball, so you wouldn't call it a comet."

"It's an asteroid. It came from the asteroid belt; you said that yourself, so it's an asteroid."

I looked back to my writing and back to her. She was nitpicking. Anyone reading it would know what I meant by "meteor." I shrugged my shoulders and moved to continue typing.

"Strictly speaking," she said, "in space you might call it a meteoroid. It's not a meteor until it enters the Earth's atmosphere. But, no one would call a rock that size a meteor. Ever."

"Someone's been spending too much time on the Internet again," I said, flashing her a smile, hoping to disarm the situation.

She snorted and then added, "Well, if you're going to write this thing you might as well get it right."

"Asteroid, meteor... who really cares? The way I have written this will work for all but the pickiest."

She crossed her arms in front of her chest and said, "Are you calling me picky?"

"Yes. Why, yes I am. Besides, I am writing this, I can write it anyway I like."

"Well then, I guess you really don't care about telling the truth of our story. If you are willing to cave on a small thing like this, what will you do when you get to the harder parts of the story?"

"You think calling an asteroid a meteor takes away from the truth of what I have written?"

"So there! You admit it is an asteroid!"

Our argument escalated from there. I saw it coming; once every two or three days we would find something to fight about. It could be little things (like asteroid versus meteor) and sometimes large things (like what the hell we were doing with our lives), but it would always be something.

The argument would take most of the day: from the spark, to the conflagration, to the smoldering silence, to the tearful makeup.

It was predictable. Like clockwork.

It was natural.

When we first moved out here I started calling it our "Fortress of Solitude," but that didn't quite fit, and it was too "Superman." This wasn't some crystal ice palace in the Arctic; this was an adobe casita in the high desert of Arizona.

So Licia suggested "Casita de Soledad," or lonely little house.

It fit, it was perfect.

So what happens when two very active, career-oriented individuals are suddenly without work and isolated? They fight.

We both knew what was happening, but we needed something to fill up the day. We were no longer saving lives or fighting supervillains. We needed something to do, didn't we?

Chapter 15

Boom Goes the Superhero
Fall 2004, Far, far above the Earth

YOU MUST REMEMBER THIS WAS IN THE EARLY DAYS. WE didn't know about the Arcturian Alliance. All the q-morphs had not been discovered yet. And Licia and I barely knew what we were capable of.

Floating there above the engines and fuel tank that had been installed on that meteor, I felt... I felt... Well, it was a bit complicated.

First was the thought that we are not alone in this universe. That, in and of itself, was a thought I rather liked. But, these beings, whoever they were, apparently wanted us dead.

So first awe, and then dread, and then fear and paranoia. I rotated myself around searching the dark void. I was sure I was being watched. Whoever did this was watching, my paranoia said. Whoever did this might retaliate if I tried to do my job.

I pushed down the paranoia, laughing it off. They obviously wanted to do this at arm's-length. They couldn't be close, could they? In hindsight, from where I sit today having been through the war, that paranoia was justified and prudent.

But there and then, I shook it off and left. I couldn't take any pictures of it to bring back, and because of the location of the structures, and the orientation of the meteor, they couldn't see this from Earth either.

I flew along the length of the meteor until I was to the middle of the long end and got to work.

I sunk into the rock, slowly. I had gauged the width of the rock in this place along its long axis. It was about 1500 feet. So, I set about sinking myself 750 feet in. I wanted to be as close to the center as I could.

I went in feet first, counting the seconds. I let the neutrino reaction spill forth from my form. Not too strong, but enough to vaporize the rock.

As my feet sunk in, the rock, now vaporized, stayed pooled like a viscous pudding. There was no gravity to speak of, there was no atmosphere, and even though we were hurtling towards the Earth at a great velocity, there was nothing to pull the vaporized rock away.

As I understand it, solar winds would eventually move the dust away from the meteor (excuse me, asteroid), but in the amount of time I looked at it, it appeared to be static.

I hadn't expected that. I fought the fear that rose up in me as the vapor got closer and closer to my head. I focused on counting. One thousand one... one thousand two... one thousand three... It took three seconds for the meteor to swallow me. I did some quick math in my head, and focused on keeping my energy output consistent. I was about six feet tall, which took three seconds. Two feet per second. At that rate, it would take about six minutes. I focused. Concentrating on my energy output, the gentle thrust from my hands forcing me down, the slow ticking away of the seconds.

It seemed like the longest six minutes of my life. When I was there, I stopped thrusting down, and rotated myself. I wanted to be aligned with the meteor. It was just a guess, but I rotated myself to what I thought was ninety degrees so that my head was now pointed at the front of the rock and my feet at the back.

It was dark and strangely peaceful in here. I paused, letting my thoughts settle. I pushed away what was at stake and concentrated on what I had to do. I brought to bear all the energy that I had absorbed in the reactor. All the energy Lightningirl had poured into me, and started the reaction.

Nuclear meltdown. Nothing less would do. Blowing this thing into chunks would do no good; all that mass would still hit the Earth. I had to vaporize the whole damn thing.

I let the reaction build and build and build. Like air being pumped into a balloon. While the energy built and the reaction cascaded, I held it in. I didn't let it go. Until—

Until I couldn't hold it anymore and the containment that was holding it (me) burst, and the energy poured out of me in a massive explosion.

THIS WAS STILL DURING THE HONEYMOON PERIOD WITH THE government and the military. This was when things were still good between us, when we q-morphs felt valued and unique. We felt like we were special, that we were needed. We didn't feel like tools being wielded by the government; we felt like participants, partners.

I didn't think of myself as a guided missile—which in many respects I was. I didn't think of myself as a weapon—which I most certainly was. I just happened to be able to do things that other people couldn't, and I was doing my part to help make the world a better place. No more, and no less, than most decent people want to do with their lives.

Don't get me wrong. If there was another meteor hurtling towards the Earth today, I would do my best to go out and try to destroy it, even if it meant the end of me. Of course I would, you would too in my situation.

And this was an unusual situation. My actions were clear with or without the military's involvement.

What I am getting at is that in those days I was still quite naïve. I was innocent and patriotic, and cynicism had not yet taken roost.

I miss those days.

Chapter 16

Neutrinoman Versus the Meteor
Fall 2004, Rocketing towards the Earth

I USED THE ANALOGY OF A BALLOON BEING FILLED UP AND popped to describe how I built up energy and released it in a massive explosion. The metaphor is apt. I felt like a popped balloon after it was over.

Consciousness fled me there for a bit. I understand what happened now, but back then I had no clue. You see, us quantum-metamorphs can change to such a degree that there really isn't any of the human "us" left. We become primal, so elemental that consciousness, as we know it, is gone. This is an extremely dangerous state for a q-morph. Extremely. All I knew was that at one moment I felt my containment of the energy failing, and the next I was floating in space, weak and spent.

I looked around, and instead of one large hunk of rock, I saw thousands upon thousands of pieces of rocks. Some the size of a fist, some the size of a cruise ship, and all sizes in between.

Eyeing it all, I estimated that I had vaporized a good 60% of the meteor, but still I was disappointed. Those larger ones could wreak havoc. If they landed on a populated area, hundreds of thousands could die.

So, weak as I was, I went back to work. There were four whoppers, and I headed towards the biggest one.

I used the same routine: sinking myself to the center, building my energy until it could not be contained and letting it tear forth out of me, vaporizing the stone.

And each time I lost consciousness again, and each time I became more exhausted.

I felt like I was playing the old Asteroids video game. I kept breaking larger rocks into smaller rocks. I kept worrying some spaceship would show up and start shooting at me.

And it was taking time. The Earth had gone from the size of a pie plate at ten feet, to filling up nearly all of my field of vision.

As I started sinking into the final whopper, I worried that I wouldn't be able to do this again. I had gone from feeling so full of energy I could hardly contain it, to feeling like a dried up husk of a man.

But there was nothing for it. So, one more time.

I sunk in; built up my energy; let it, much diminished as it was, explode forth.

I knew nothing for quite some time until I felt the atmosphere, cold and biting, tearing at my naked flesh. Until I felt my lungs empty and desperately sucking for oxygen that wasn't there. Until I knew that my neutrino form had fled me and I was sure I was going to die.

IT WAS THE SUN THAT SAVED ME.

I don't know if it was the neutrino emissions, the UV-A

or UV-B or some other type of solar radiation, but it was the sun that saved me.

As I felt the cold biting into me, the thin air starting to tug at me, I looked up at the sun. It was bright, so bright, a placid yellow orb, eternal, fixed, unchanging.

The air cooled me, but the sun warmed me. I drank it in. I gave myself over to it. Just as my lungs burned with a pain beyond bearing; just as I thought my flesh would freeze and be torn from my body, I changed.

The sun, unfiltered as it is on the ground, gave me just enough radiation to change back to my neutrino form. I couldn't fly, I could barely move. But I didn't feel the cold, the thin air no longer bit into me, my lungs, no longer lungs, didn't need oxygen.

I fell then, amidst the remnants of the meteor, I fell.

As the atmosphere became denser, the rocks started to glow and trailed fire. They started to dissolve as we streaked towards the surface below.

I looked around, briefly interested, but then turned my attention back to the sun. The more I focused on it, the better I felt.

As the atmosphere started to occlude the sun's radiation from me, I turned my attention back homeward.

We tumbled through the air, the rocks and me, in a large group as far as I could see.

Most were small, but some were still the size of houses, and although I felt myself coming back, I didn't have enough energy to do anything about it.

I stared below me trying to get my bearings. I wasn't over Arizona anymore. It looked like I would be coming down in the Pacific. I wasn't sure, from my altitude now somewhere in the stratosphere, it looked like it would be an ocean landing.

And at first I was fine with that. I couldn't hurt anyone. But there would be no help for me either.

I turned east, towards my home, and with what little energy I had, I thrusted.

It came in spurts and sputters, but it was enough to change my trajectory.

As the clouds came closer and closer, I saw a glimpse of the fighter jets, the SR-71 Blackbirds running at the highest altitude. What caught my attention was seeing one of them explode; one of the meteors must have hit it. I was still far away and I continued to thrust for all I was worth.

When I saw the second set of jets, I wasn't as far off, and this time one didn't need to explode for me to see them.

I gave one last push, all of my energy exiting out my feet, moving me back into my expected flight path, and then I knew nothing again.

Interlude 4

Motives

Spring 2025, Casita de Soledad, Central Arizona

I DIDN'T NEED TO LOOK TO KNOW SHE WAS THERE, I COULD feel her behind me; I could sense her electrical presence. She was shifting slowly from her left foot to her right foot and back. She was reading what I had just written.

"Yes?" I asked, without turning around. I could feel her question too.

"Why, exactly, are you doing this?" she asked, her tone even, her words loaded.

"We've been over this," I said as I swiveled in my chair to face her. "I think our true story needs to be told. There is so much misinformation about us and the other q-morphs, about the war and what happened."

She nodded slowly. She wasn't buying it. "And..."

"And?"

"And what are your other reasons? Is it that you are just bored with retirement? Miss the 'good ole days' and need to relive them through writing them down?"

I paused. What she said had merit, but it didn't feel right. I shook my head, "No."

"Then?" she prompted.

"Then what? Do I need more of a reason than telling our story?"

She paused, her eyes searching me. "Yes, you do. I know you; you need more of a reason than that."

I sighed and nodded. She was right. I didn't really think it was just setting the record straight, or just ego. It was—

"Our love story needs to be told," I said with a smile. "You yourself said that was the place to start."

She smiled back with a nod. "And?"

"And what!" I was growing exasperated, but I knew her well enough to know she wouldn't stop digging until she found what she was after.

"Is it about him?" she asked, her voice barely above a whisper.

That brought me up short, fear growing in my belly. I hadn't thought about it yet; he was a huge part of this story, but—

"I'm not ready to even think about him yet," I snapped. "Not even to think about thinking about him."

"So that's it then?" she asked. "That's the 'and'?"

I felt my cheeks flush red and nodded, turning back to my writing.

Chapter 17

Landing

Fall 2004, Entering the atmosphere

An intense roaring sound, like an untuned radio turned all the way up, stuck in my ears. Cold tugging at my flesh like I had been thrust in frigid arctic waters. Pain tearing through my lungs as they sucked for oxygen; this time finding it, but not enough.

A fiery crackling pain in my chest. A noise so sharp and loud I was sure my eardrums would burst. The sharp smell of ozone. Energy coursing back through me. Life returning to me as my neutrino form flickered back on.

The ground rising up at an alarming rate to meet me. Several ponds of dark inky water, round buildings, and a nest of spindly sliver towers and wires.

Flesh returns as the ground nears. Searing crackling pain in my back. Neutrino form comes back.

Impact. The ground explodes around me and swallows me. Flesh returns, unbearable pain. Darkness.

Chapter 18

Recuperation

Fall 2004, Luke Air Force Base, Arizona

I HEARD FIRST: A STEADY BEEPING, LOUD AND SHRILL. I smelled next: the sharp tang of antiseptic. I felt then: deep throbbing pain masked by a light floating sensation that made me feel nauseous.

I heard a moan and realized it was me making the noise. I felt a warm squeeze of my hand.

"Nik... Nik..." A feminine voice. Light, like meringue; silky and smooth. Rich and delicate and strong, with an undertone that seemed out of place: fatigue and fear.

I heard myself moan again and tried to open my eyes, but they wouldn't obey me. They felt glued shut.

"Nik. Oh thank God." I felt the warmth squeezing my hand again and felt the barest tingle of electricity. I heard the sound of crying. I tried to soak in the warmth like I soaked in the sun while I was falling earthward.

My eyes obeyed me when I tried to open them next. A face, round and smiling, framed by long black hair. Thick eyebrows, brown eyes, tears running down the cheeks of that face. Lips pale and drawn, white teeth pressing down on their lower lip.

"Licia..." I groaned.

"Nik, you're okay. We are in a hospital."

"Meteor?"

"You did it, Nik, you did it."

"We..." I said weakly.

"We?"

"*We* did it." I remembered those lightning bolts striking me as I plunged towards the Earth. That energy had let me be neutrino again; those lightning bolts had save my life. "*You* saved me."

She laughed then, it escaped her as if it had been trapped and under pressure too long. It wasn't an easy laugh, it was full of pain and strife, but it was laughter. I liked it.

"Zap me."

She laughed again, this time easier and lighter, but still weighty.

"Does this mean there's going to be a second date?" I asked. This time her laughter rang out bright and clear. I rode its blissful rhythm back into unconsciousness.

I BEGGED THEM TO TAKE ME TO THE REACTOR, OR TO LET Licia zap me, but they wouldn't. They said I wasn't stable enough to move, that the danger was too great, that my injuries were too extensive.

And they were extensive. Broken pelvis, left arm, and left leg; broken ribs and collapsed lung; concussion; frostbite; and various bruises and lacerations.

I had been my neutrino self when I hit the ground, right on the edge of the transformer towers, right behind the power plant. That had saved my life. My impact dug a crater fifteen feet deep in the ground, throwing sand and rock for hundreds of yards.

I also took out half of the relay towers, plunging two states and millions of customers into darkness for a week. It was officially a "terrorist attack" linked to the missile attack on the helicopter. But, I felt bad for that and for—

While I had vaporized and broken up most of the meteor into small enough sizes so they burned up in the atmosphere, there were still some sizeable chunks. There was great destruction and damage.

A chunk the size of a bus struck in downtown Los Angeles taking out the US Bank Tower and some surrounding high-rises. The biggest remaining piece landed about fifty miles out in the Pacific, creating a mini-tsunami that caught much of the West Coast unawares. There were smaller pieces, from the size of a baseball to the size of a bowling ball, that came down all across the Desert Southwest and California. One of those chunks entered through the capstone of the Luxor in Las Vegas. Another blasted the historic Pima County Courthouse in Tucson. But, the Desert Southwest being as sparsely populated as it is, most of them didn't do any real harm.

But I felt bad. Bad that I hadn't done a better job. Bad that there were so many deaths. The death toll eventually climbed to 24,389—most of them in LA. I tell myself that it could have been—would have been—much, much worse without me. But I still feel for all those who died and their families.

Lying in bed waiting for my bones to heal gave me way too much time to think about it.

MY MOM WAS THERE THE SECOND TIME I WOKE UP. I FELT warmth in my hand, but it felt different, the hand felt fatter. I opened my eyes hoping for Licia and found my mom staring at me. She was in bad shape: dark circles under her eyes, her normally well-groomed hair flat and oily, brown and grey roots vigorously pushing out the blond.

"Al," she croaked, calling for my father. "Al, he's awake."

I smiled around the pain. I wanted to show her that I was okay. "How'd the Cardinals do yesterday?" I wanted to distract her.

She shook her head. "The Cardinals played last Sunday, six days ago. You've been out for a while."

I found out we were at a facility on Luke Air Force Base, so I knew the doctor had clearance and he confirmed this when he told me he knew who I was. That is when I found out they had no plans of transporting me back to Palo Verde anytime soon.

"I am sorry, sir, you are too weak," he said.

"Weak? Yeah I'm weak. Put me in a nice radiation bath and I'll get strong, fast."

"I am sorry, sir. Orders."

And that was that. It was the military, after all. There didn't need to be logic or reason, just "orders."

I had a suspicion that going q-morph would more than help. I believed it would heal me and quick. I had experienced it before on a small scale. At that point, I had morphed once with the flu, and once with a sprained ankle. In both cases, my ailment did not come back when I returned to my physical form.

They knew this, I had mentioned it in debriefs, but it had never been investigated or acted on. It was not part of my official dossier. So, no, they wouldn't let me go. They wouldn't take a chance on this. I was way too valuable. And that just made me mad.

The next time I awoke it was to the angular face and brush-cut of Colonel Williams. No one was holding my hand. No one else was there except for round-faced General Markus, and the door was closed.

"On behalf of a grateful nation and world, I thank you," General Markus said. "You do understand, of course, that these events are, and must remain, top secret."

His little speech just relit my anger. Barely conscious and some old-fart general is lecturing me on keeping his secrets, reminding me that I am a prisoner in his hospital.

Maybe it was the drugs; maybe it was my mood. But, come on, I had just saved the world. I expected more than that. It was clear that they would want me to keep my mouth shut, go back to my janitor job (and janitor salary) and act like nothing had happened. They were keeping me stuck in this bed when a short trip to Palo Verde would do me wonders.

"I want access to the reactor. Now," I said. I meant it to sound like a command, but my voice was weak and it came out as a croak.

"The doctors have advised against it," Williams said.

"It will help," I said.

"The risk is too high."

"The risk is mine to take."

"I am afraid not, son," Markus said. It grated on my nerves, him calling me "son." I wasn't his son. "If something goes wrong, if you are not strong enough to handle the radiation, to contain it... well, that would be catastrophic."

"I'm sorry, Nik," Colonel Williams interjected. He, at

least, I believed. "You're just going to have to tough this out for a while longer."

I nodded. I didn't like it, but I can't say that I wasn't a little bit worried about it too. It was unknown territory.

"Can I get some time in the sun at least?" I asked, remembering how the sun had saved me when I had been in orbit.

Williams nodded. "Now, can you tell us what happened?"

The debrief was short, and I'm not sure if they believed me when I told them about the structure on the meteor. But at that point I didn't care. The sun, I would get to be in the sun soon. The sun would give me what I needed.

My recuperation was very slow, until it wasn't. I was in the hospital for another three weeks. When they finally let me into the reactor, I rolled in on a wheelchair and walked out with a cane. It wasn't instantaneous, it still took a long time, but morphing did speed up my healing.

And as I grew stronger and stronger one thing—or rather, one person—was on my mind. Licia Lopez. It felt true. It felt right. It felt like Ashley and all that coasting after her departure was over. I finally knew who I was. I knew who I wanted to be. I knew who I wanted to be with.

Chapter 19

A Second Date
Fall 2004, Page Springs Cellars, Arizona

WE SAT AT A PICNIC TABLE ON A DECK THAT OVERLOOKED Oak Creek on one of those weirdly warm fall days Arizona can have. We had finally made it to that little winery in the Verde Valley. There was a bottle of wine from the winery (a lovely red wine called El Serrano), a red and white checkered tablecloth, a plate of assorted cheeses, and some crackers.

And there was Licia. She had her dark hair tied back and was dressed casually in a red tank top and some khaki shorts. The shirt was emblazoned with the Flash Gordon logo: a white circle in the middle of the red with a yellow lightning bolt going through it. I loved it. It was her. A sly embrace of who she was and a not-so-sly thumbing at the authority that was just starting to feel oppressive.

I watched her as she talked, her face expressive and animated. Her hands darting out to take a piece of cheese and then delicately putting it on a cracker, as if apologetic for depriving me of even one morsel of the stuff. I watched how she laughed with her eyes, almost more than her face.

We spoke in hushed tones. We were alone, it was in the middle of the day in the middle of the week, but we didn't want to be overheard. Not all of it was talk of powers and saving the world. Our tones were hushed even with the most mundane of matters. Like, how she loved to watch reruns of the TV show *Buffy the Vampire Slayer*, and how I loved to watch really bad sci-fi movies on lazy days off.

The surroundings seemed to support us. The creek below provided pleasant white noise; the tall cottonwoods guarded us as they swayed in the gentle breeze; the grapevines in the vineyard above watched respectfully.

Towards the end, after I had poured the last bits of wine into our glasses, she leaned over the table, stretching towards me like a flower reaching for the sun. Without thinking I stretched towards her too, and as our lips came close, tendrils of yellow neutronic energy stabbed from my lips to hers as sparks of electricity jumped from hers to mine. And all of the sudden—

We were kissing. Our first kiss. That last few inches happened so fast, as if the energy exchange had acted like a magnet, drawing our lips together. It was a relatively chaste kiss, just lips, but I felt it to the soles of my feet.

It was electrical, yes. But somehow, it was something more. It was as if my life began in that moment. As if her soft lips pressed against mine, her breath smelling of wine and cheese, breathed life into me for the very first time.

We were interrupted by our phones going off simultaneously. Hers played "Flash a-ah ..."; a tiny snippet from the theme song from the 1980 movie *Flash Gordon*. It went perfectly with her shirt.

Mine played a snippet from "I Don't Wanna Miss a Thing" from Armageddon. It was my (way too subtle) thumbing at authority.

She groaned and held her phone to me, it said: "Report

to PV ASAP." I laughed and showed her my phone—it said the same thing.

"I guess it's time to save the world again," I said with a shrug.

Our first kiss didn't last that long. And you know what, it didn't need to. It was all I could have wished for. A perfect second date.

Epilogue

Spring 2025, Casita de Soledad, Central Arizona

I SAT IN A CHAIR OUTSIDE OUR CASITA ON OUR FLAGSTONE patio, absorbing the rays of the sun directly above. It had been a long time since I had had access to reactor number three at Palo Verde Nuclear Generating Station. I missed it. The sun was the next best thing available.

I heard the pages turn every minute or so. A soft quiet whisper as Licia read the story I had just completed. She had insisted that I print it out. She was afraid if she tried to read it on the e-reader she might get "emotional" and fry the thing.

I was dressed only in shorts so I could get as much solar radiation as possible. Despite my several hours a day of this, my skin was as white as a sheet. My body absorbed the UV differently than most.

A silence had descended—the turning of pages had ended some minutes ago—and it filled up the space between us. I wanted to ask, but I didn't. I let the silence deepen. She just needed a moment to gather her thoughts.

I heard her sniff and turned to look at her. Her eyes were

moist and she had been crying. I felt that sinking feeling I feel every time she cries. It didn't matter if it was a "good" cry or a "bad" cry (I usually couldn't tell the difference), it always scared me.

"Honey?" I asked.

She looked at me and said, "Oh, don't worry. It's beautiful, it's perfect. It's a good start, and I am glad you are doing this. I am."

"Why are you crying?"

"We were so innocent back then."

I nodded; we really were. We had just saved the world and we were falling in love, but really, we had no idea what was about to happen.

She rose from her chair, hopped off the deck, and extended her hand to me. "Let's go for a walk."

We walked up a well-worn path that wound around our property and up onto a hill. From there we could see far: the flat top of the Mogollon Rim to the north; the undulating hills of the high desert we lived in; and the dips of canyons to the east. The grasses were a pale green with the first flush of spring, and the sky was a piercing blue. It was beautiful.

It was also isolating. I love the desert, with all my heart, but the life we were living, it was... it was isolated, yes, but worse, it was small. We had lived as large a life as we could, and now nearly as small a life as we could.

Licia had been right when she had asked me why I was writing this. It is more than just telling our story, setting the record straight. It's coming to grips with my life, and where we've ended up.

Licia led me on and lost in thought, I didn't notice as we approached the power lines. It was a major electrical artery, running from Glen Canyon Dam down to Phoenix.

It was one of the reasons we had chosen this place for our "retirement." Licia needed access to power.

Back from the towers, about fifty yards, was a cheap metal shed. Inside were a few hooks on the wall and nothing else. As we approached it, she saw the question on my face.

She shrugged, her shoulders playing with her long black hair, "It's been too long."

I nodded. It was a sweet gesture, really. To this day she doesn't like to fly and after all we have been through, I can't blame her.

We went into the shed, took our clothes off, hung them on the hooks there and walked a few yards closer to the tower where a flagstone circle, about ten feet in diameter, had been created. We call it the "launching pad."

"Ready?" she asked, a smile playing about her lips. I was staring at her body and she knew it. Even after all these years I can't help myself; she's gorgeous. Part of it is natural and part of it is all this quantum morphing we do; we are aging slowly. It's been over twenty years since we met and she looks about five years older.

I nodded, "Ready."

She extended her left hand to the tower, fingers out. Electricity arced from the power line, meeting her fingers and her body. Her curves turn from flesh to electrical as she turns from human to q-morph, from Licia to Lightningirl.

I felt my body responding, without even thinking. I'd soaked up enough solar radiation to power my own transformation. I looked down as my white flesh turned into the swirling yellow of my neutrino form.

A white bolt of electricity arced from her extended right palm and hit me in the chest.

We were a bit out of practice, but we were much better

at this than in the old days. It was intense but felt good. Felt familiar. I smiled.

We stood there for some minutes as she poured energy into me. I felt that old feeling of power coursing through me. God, how I had missed it.

When I was pulsing and glowing, she stopped the transfer and walked up to me. She delicately put her arms around my neck and gently stepped on top of my feet. I put my arms around her waist, pulling her close, and she giggled as our quantum forms pressed against each other. Yellow tendrils arcing from me to her as white tendrils arced from her to me. Our bodies dance in a positive feedback loop that makes us, together, more than we could possibly be apart.

I looked into her electrical eyes and she gave me a small smile and a smaller nod.

We surged into the air, the ground retreating below us.

I knew that they'd know, of course. That they'd want an accounting of our use of our powers. But right then I didn't care, right then I was doing exactly what I needed.

Licia was right, it had been too long.

Want more of the adventures of Neutrinoman and Lightningirl? The following is a sample of Episode #2.

Toxic Asset

Neutrinoman & Lightningirl
A Love Story

Episode #2

Chapter 1

The Realized Romantic
Fall 2004, Page Springs Cellars, Arizona

It would be pretty easy to classify me as a hopeless romantic. And back then, back when Licia/Lightningirl and I met, I would have agreed with you. Ashley's abrupt departure years earlier had stalled both my professional life and my romantic life, but I was still the same romantic fool I always was--with the scars to prove it.

But now, from the perspective of where I sit today? Nope, not in the least.

Am I a romantic? Yes, guilty as charged. But I am no longer hopeless. Actually, it's really an annoying term isn't it? Hopeless Romantic. It describes the person who constantly seeks love but never achieves it. I don't know about you, but that sounds like a hopeful romantic. Charging in time and again to let love (or the mere hope of love) kick your teeth in, seems to require hope.

So back then, I was actually a hopeful romantic. Now? Having been in a relationship with the same woman for several decades and still being in love? I am a realized romantic. Not that love doesn't still kick my teeth in (metaphorically speaking, of course). It does. And it does it regularly. Sorry to break the news to all you romantics that are still hopeful--love, she's a tough mistress.

Anyway, back at the winery nestled in the Verde Valley when we had our first kiss, back when our lips first met, back when a mere pressing of her flesh against mine could rock me to my soul, back when that phone call had interrupted the most perfect second date--I was crestfallen. I was having the time of my life and now some damn world-threatening emergency was interfering.

Licia, who no one would ever describe as a romantic (hopeless, hopeful, or otherwise), saw it on my face. I was still sitting at the picnic table after she had gathered our wine glasses and empty wine bottle, folded the red and white checkered tablecloth, and had taken it all ten paces towards the winery. She realized I wasn't walking with her, turned around, and said, "It's okay, Nik. We'll have more time. I promise."

She walked back and set the basket down. A romantic she may not be, but she was always perceptive.

"It was perfect... This was perfect," I said, looking around us at the creek below, the vines above, the beautiful blue sky, and the oddly warm fall day.

Her brown eyes narrowed as she took a slow breath and let it out, pulling her silky black hair back into a ponytail. "Look. Let's not give it up yet. They want us both down at Palo Verde, right?" I nodded. We had been summoned back to my home base--Palo Verde Nuclear Generating Station west of Phoenix. "So we'll ride together. That will give us another two hours." She ended the sentence with a dazzling smile, her hand resting on mine jolting me with a trickle of energy as our bodies did their thing.

My doldrums vanquished, I grabbed the basket and started running towards the large white building that housed the wine cellar below and the tasting room above. "Race you!" I shouted as I ran past her.

WE STOOD IN THE DIRT PARKING LOT OF THE WINERY, THE rolling desert hills of Arizona's wine country rising up around us. We were looking at our cars. Mine was a beat-up 1990 Ford Focus that was a faded blue that might have been pretty before the Arizona sun bleached it out, and at this point might look decent if I washed it more than once every two years. Hers was a 2002 four-wheel-drive Toyota pickup. It was a shiny black, clean as could be, and beautiful.

We both stood there looking from car to truck to car. She was really being kind. It was obvious we should take the truck. But since we were still, officially, on a date, I kind of thought I should drive. She knew this, I knew this, but I just stood there, my mind mush as I tried to figure out a graceful way through this. Sure, the world might be ending any moment and we had been summoned by the powers that be. Sure, I knew that, but there I stood, my head going from left to right trying to find a way to preserve my dignity.

And this may be old fashioned, this desire to drive my date, but hey, what can I say? I'm kind of like that.

"Nik..." she began, "we're kind of in a hurry."

"Right," I said, my head still going from left to right and back. "That sure is a nice truck."

"Thanks."

It made sense. I was paid a janitor's salary, and she was a linewoman for the local electricity provider, APS. I lived at home; she lived alone. It made sense, there was a reason her vehicle was much nicer than mine. Except for the dirty part, of course--I just hate to wash cars (and make beds), the effort doesn't yield results long enough to seem worth it to me.

Licia brought her hand to my shoulder and the tingle there jiggled my brain enough for something to occur to me. "We're in a hurry, right?" I asked.

"Yup."

"Well, then, we better take your truck. I am almost out of gas, and we definitely don't have time to stop."

"We definitely don't," she said, her voice suitably serious.

We both stood there for a few more breaths. I am not sure why. Maybe we were both afraid of what it meant. Man and Woman on a second date kiss for the first time. Man is the romantic one, Woman is the practical one. Emergency strikes and Man and Woman must think and act fast. They both get into Woman's superior vehicle and ride off to save the day.

I was just not sure it was the right precedent to set so early in a relationship. Nevertheless, we got in, her driving, and went down Page Springs Road towards Cornville, heading towards I-17 and Phoenix.

We hadn't gone very far when there was a ringing from her glove compartment. "It's the batphone," Licia said with a smile, "you better get it."

Batphone? What was she talking about? I, of course, understood the reference. On the old Batman TV show, Commissioner Gordon had this special red phone that Batman called him on in emergencies.

I opened the glove compartment and there was a black satellite phone. Circa 2004, they were still pretty big. Licia must have seen the puzzled look on my face because she said, "You don't have one of those? It's military spec, encrypted, secure."

I was still puzzled but answered the phone, "Hello." Seems kind of lame, huh? Here I am answering the equivalent of the batphone and that is all I come up with. Hello-lame.

"Who is this?" the gravelly voice on the phone said. "This phone is government property and should be in the possession of Licia Lopez. Who is this?"

The voice sounded familiar, but I couldn't quite place it. After my lame greeting, I wasn't about to comply. "Who is this?" I said, my lightning wit clearly on the fritz.

"This is Colonel Williams of the United States Army. State your name now or there will be consequences."

"Oh. Hi, Colonel Williams. This is Nik, Nik Nichols."

"Nichols? What are you doing with Ms. Lopez's phone?"

"We were together when the call came in and decided to head down to Palo Verde together."

"Oh... Um..." the older man stuttered. "What... What were you two doing together?"

I didn't particularly like the question. Wasn't the world ending or something? Hadn't we received an urgent call? "Um... drinking wine, Colonel."

"What? Really? You and Ms. Lopez?"

Now I was getting angry. "Yes sir, me and Ms. Lopez were enjoying an alcoholic beverage together. Isn't there an urgent matter to attend to?"

"Yes... Well... We'll talk about this later." His voice resumed its normal authoritative baritone as he continued. "Put this on speaker since you're both there."

I did as ordered.

"Ms. Lopez, Mr. Nichols, we have a bit of an emergency.

The situation has escalated since we called you in, and we need you on site ASAP."

"Yes, sir," Licia said. "Can you fill us in on the nature of the situation?"

"It's Toxicwasteman," Colonel Williams said. I saw Licia tense up and her knuckles go white on the steering wheel. "He's escaped the Florence prison and commandeered a semi full of chemicals and got himself reactivated." Just like electricity enables Licia to turn into Lightningirl and radiation lets me turn into Neutrinoman, Tom Tyree needs toxic substances to turn him into Toxicwasteman.

"I hate that guy," Licia said through gritted teeth. "I just hate that guy."

"We caught up with him," Williams continued, "but he's taken some hostages in a little place called Green Valley, south of Tucson. There's a standoff. He says he will release them if he gets to talk to Neutrinoman."

"What? Me?" I asked, shocked.

"Yes, Nik. You. Something is wrong with him. He's been babbling about aliens and the threat from Arcturus. The media is going to be there soon, and we can't have him scaring people."

I was shocked. The colonel seemed more worried about him talking to the media than if he killed the hostages. And why would Toxicwasteman want to talk to me? And what, or where, the hell is Arcturus?

Back then I was clueless. Now, we all know that Arcturus is a star, the brightest star in the Boötes constellation, and the home system of the Arcturian Alliance.

"Licia," he continued, "you know Toxicwasteman better than anyone, I--"

"Well I should," Licia said, "I am the one who put him in that prison. How the hell did he get out?"

"Don't know, but we are investigating. As I was saying, I want both of you on site ASAP. It's a diner called Big Al's right off of I-19 south of Tucson on the way to Nogales. What is your location now?"

"We are on Cornville Road a few miles west of I-17," Licia said.

"Okay. Nik, what are your energy levels like?"

"Not so great, sir," I said. "I haven't been in the reactor for about a week."

"Here's what we're going to do," Colonel Williams said as he laid out his plan.

Chapter 2

Piggy-back Ride
Fall 2004, Central, Arizona

Licia pulled the truck over and parked next to the road. There was a small bridge that drained water from a side canyon into Beaver Creek just behind us and that would have to do. We dumped the contents of our pockets under the seats. Licia locked the truck and put the keys under a nearby rock. We scrambled down the shoulder and under the bridge.

"Umm..." I began, eying my clothing and hers, knowing they would be burned off when we changed into our superhero forms. I didn't say anything else, just pointed at my clothing and then hers.

"Boys' side," she said pointing to the far side of the culvert.

I went to the designated area, my back to Licia, took my clothes off, and changed into my neutrino form. "Ready?" I asked when I was done, keeping my back turned.

"Yes, let's get moving."

I turned and gasped. Not that I hadn't seen her as Lightningirl before, but something about the intimacy of our outing and my inherent romantic nature amplified it for me. The cement walls were lit up brightly with the blue-white light of her coruscating electrical form. She was gorgeous: petite, well proportioned, and very feminine.

I walked over to her, the yellow light of my neutrino form mixed with the blue-white of her lightning form and danced on the cement walls. We walked to the edge of the tunnel, where she moved to stand on my feet and assume the "slow dance" position we had used when we had flown before.

"Sorry, that's not going to work," I said. With her fear of flying, I hated to break it to her.

"What?"

"I am going to need my hands. We're not going straight up. I will need both my hands and feet to fly us."

"Oh," she said, her electric face scrunched.

I turned my back to her and squatted a bit. "Piggyback. It's the only way."

I was facing out of the tunnel and couldn't see her. After a few moments of silence, I turned around. Her arms were crossed and a frown was on her face.

"You're not messing with me, are you?" she asked.

I held up my hands. "No. God no. If we are going straight up I can manage that with my feet. But we are going to be flying like this," I put my hand out so it was about 15 degrees angled up from horizontal. "I am going to need my hands to keep us steady."

"Oh... Well... Wait. Why can't you shoot those yellow jets out of other parts of your body?"

I started to laugh, imagining what other parts of my body to shoot jets out of, but cut it short when I saw her face. She was perfectly serious. "I guess I could, but I've never tried before, and I don't think this is the time."

She nodded, fear returning to her face quickly replaced by stony resolve.

"Okay then," she said, waving for me to "assume the position."

I went back to the edge of the tunnel and squatted. She hopped on my back, her arms wrapping tightly around my chest and her thighs clamping my waist. I put my arms down straight and pressed them against her legs holding them firmly against me.

As I was about to take off, it occurred to me why she thought I might be messing with her. We were in our quantum forms, which meant we were, to all intents and purposes, naked, which made this arrangement pretty intimate.

I took us up into the air quickly, angling us out of the tunnel and up at an angle slightly to the south. The idea was to limit our exposure to witnesses. Once we were up about five thousand feet, I took us past the Verde Valley and south to the large mesa that sits between the Verde Valley and the Phoenix Area.

There is a set of high-tension power lines that runs from the northern edge of Arizona, at Glen Canyon Dam, all the way south to Phoenix; that was our destination.

This area is high desert, with beautiful rolling hills and canyons. It is a magical area that I always love driving through.

Once I thought we were in the right place, I brought us down quickly, adjusting our trajectory as the power lines came into view. We didn't know it then, but we were very close to where Casita de Soledad would someday be.

When we were about a thousand feet up, I felt my energy failing--the neutrino jets that were keeping us aloft started to sputter out.

"Woops," I said as we suddenly started to drop.

"Got it," Licia said as she removed her left hand from my chest extending it towards the power lines that were rapidly approaching. Electricity arced from them to her left hand and from her right hand into my chest.

Properly powered, I landed us gracefully next to the power lines. She got off my back, I turned to face her, and she directed the electricity into my chest. We did this for about ten minutes until I was feeling powerful enough to get us down past Tucson.

It wasn't comfortable, the lightning bolt she was directing into me, but I enjoyed the moment because we were still alone.

"YOU OKAY?" I ASKED AS WE SOARED HIGH ABOVE PHOENIX. Her grip around my chest was a bit tight. Well no, to be honest, it was very tight.

"Uh huh," she mumbled. It was what I have come to fondly call her yes-no. She said "yes," but she meant "no." It wasn't the words, but the delivery. It's often more subtle than that, but even a dolt like me could tell she wasn't having a good time.

"Not too much longer," I lied. Well, I guess the magnitude of the lie depends on how much is "not too much." Clearly we were already past her limit, so any longer would be too much longer for her.

And I think maybe it was the mode of flying. When we had dealt with the meteor (excuse me, asteroid), we had flown straight up. For this we were flying almost horizontally. She was basically lying on me as I flew us. She had nowhere to look but down.

It took us about forty minutes to do the 250 miles. So we were going fast, but forty minutes is a long time when you hate flying. Even more so when you hate flying and you're holding on to a controlled nuclear reaction with nothing to protect you but said nuclear reaction.

So yeah, she was holding on to me pretty tight. I can't say that I minded in the least.

I could have gotten us there faster, but I thought nearly 400 mph was fast enough. This type of flight was new for both of us. I also kept I-17, then I-10 and I-19 in sight. Even though I had spent quite a bit of time studying maps after I learned how to fly, I wasn't ready to attempt a straight, as the superhero flies, route. I don't have any technological navigational aids, and I didn't want to get lost.

"So, umm..." I began, speaking loudly so she could hear me clearly. "So, did you go to high school in Flagstaff?" I was trying to distract her.

"Yeah," she answered without elaboration.

"Born there?"

"No. New Mexico. My dad moved us out when I was young."

That was better. At least I got a sentence that time. "How come?"

"Construction. Flag was growing a lot back in the 80s, lot of opportunity for him."

And so it went, soaring ten thousand feet above the Desert Southwest, the dry and rugged landscape passing below us. I did my best to distract her. When her answers got short I would change topics. For example, I learned that she doesn't like ice cream (who knew that was possible?); is an avid rock climber (Flagstaff's a pretty good place for that); loves to get pedicures (she is a girl, I know, but an

APS linewoman and rock climber--I wasn't expecting that); and can't stand romantic comedies (that was, given my romantic nature, a disappointment).

As we skirted to the east of Phoenix, Colonel Williams had cleared a flight path for us, I asked, "So why are you a vegetarian?" I had noticed this the night we had met at dinner at my folks' house. That one act of perception had been important in our relationship getting this far.

"Is that a problem?" she countered.

"No, not at all. Just curious."

She was silent for a while and I was about to change subjects when she said, "A failure to have compassion for one species of animal, but not for others."

"What?"

"I love dogs. When we got to Flag, the family got a dog. He was a coyote-mix rescue from the reservation. I loved that dog: he played and howled and loved to tromp through the forest with me. His name was Jake--he adored me and I adored him. He saw me all the way through high school before his poor old body gave out."

She was silent then, and I let it be for a bit. I knew I had just learned something important about her. This vegetarian backstory was clearly a big deal.

"So..." I said, trying to wrap my head around it. "Because you love Jake, you can't eat cows?" I frankly didn't understand, but that is as well as I could state it.

"Exactly," she said. I could hear the smile in her voice. I dropped the subject, which was wise, considering that just because I said it didn't mean I understood it. In love, it is often best to quit while you are ahead.

When we got past Tucson and were headed south above I-19, two Apache Attack helicopters showed up and escorted us in.

Chapter 3

A Sip of Fame
Fall 2004, Green Valley, Arizona

WHEN WE WERE GETTING CLOSE TO OUR DESTINATION, IT became obvious. The TV vans with their big satellite dishes on their roofs, the cop cars with their lights flashing, the dark green tents, and assembled military vehicles made it obvious.

The place the helicopters guided us to was about fifty yards away from "Big Al's Truck Stop and Gas Station." I liked it instantly upon seeing it. It was a relic from another era. One of those greasy spoon diners with a long bar you can eat at and a bunch of gas pumps out front.

It was like going back in time. Somehow this little place had survived and kept its character despite the homogenization of the commercial world.

"A little power," I said as I positioned us vertically, arresting our forward motion, and started a gentle descent. I saw a power line close by and was running low on juice.

This was an important day for Lightningirl and me. This was our first tiny sip of fame, our first encounter with the media. This was the first time that we were being filmed close up.

When I saw the lightning arc from the power line and felt the power flow into me, I breathed a sigh of relief. I really had no grasp of what fame was like, or the crazy pressure it puts on you, I just didn't want to screw up in front of the cameras. And, you know, I had good reason to worry about my landings. There were many craters that marked my poorer attempts.

NO SOONER HAD WE LANDED THAN WE WERE RUSHED INTO a big green army tent. We both tightened containment on our respective reactions (nuclear and electrical) so no one would be exposed to too much radiation and no electrical equipment would get fried. It wouldn't work long-term but was good enough for a quick briefing.

"Any trouble getting here?" Colonel Williams asked, his angular face looking longer than usual.

"No, sir," Lightningirl said.

"Good. Good. We don't have much time. We need to get you two in there. Your priority is to keep Toxicwasteman from talking to the media."

"What?" I was angry. Sure Williams was a military guy, answers to orders and all that, but I had come to rely on a shred of humanity always showing through. "Our priority is not the hostages? Not to save lives?"

Colonel Williams looked at me unblinking for a few moments, his hand worrying at his salt-and-pepper brush-cut hair. "Yes, lives are the priority, but you've got to keep in mind the big picture. If he talks too much about aliens, if it gets out, if people panic... Well, there are a lot more lives at stake than the dozen hostages in there."

After the briefing, we made "The Walk." It was a pathway

made by military personnel and highway patrol through a thicket of media about twenty yards long.

As we left the tent, Williams shouted, "And don't talk to the media!" The seemingly endless sea of cameras, microphones, and reporters were enough to make me never want to talk again. It was late afternoon but still the cameras' flashes were going off, accompanying the shouts from the reporters. It was like this assemblage of oddly limbed, one-eyed cyclops following our every move.

I hated it. We both did.

And most of the questions they asked were just stupid: "How do you think Toxicwasteman escaped?" as if we would know; "How does it feel to be a national hero?" as if I could express the potent cocktail of joy and horror that make it up; "Lightningirl, what do you think about the trend of skirts getting shorter?" as if that had any relevance to anyone anywhere; and "Is that his... his... his thing there?" yes, ladies and gentlemen, that is the neutronic version of my genitals--sorry a costume is just not an option when you're a contained nuclear reaction, as much as I would like it to be.

That last comment left me deeply humiliated and deeply self-conscious, and kind of was my first initiation to what fame was going to be like. Because that's what it is like: walking around naked with people talking about you in intimate detail like you are not there.

Lightningirl and I were walking close together. The interaction between our two forms was evident and would be much speculated for months to come. I frankly found her electrical presence comforting as we walked down that very long twenty yards. I was beginning to hope for a meteor to go intercept, at least then I wouldn't have my every move and facial expression analyzed.

Right at the end, just when I thought we would make it, I heard, "Neutrinoman, are you and Lightningirl together?"

I stopped and looked, my head seeking the source of the sound. Lightningirl kept walking as if she hadn't heard (she, to this day, claims she didn't, but I have my doubts).

When my eyes found the reporter, they stayed there. She was beautiful, but in that "too beautiful to be real" way that TV reporters often are. She had shiny black hair that cascaded over her shoulders in gentle waves, red lips, and green eyes. "Green" is not a fair way to describe them. Her eyes were luminous, as if lit by some inner light.

"Are you?" she asked, pointing a microphone towards me, the rapid fire clicking and flashing of the cameras overwhelming. "Are you together?" I would later find out that her name was Diane Madison, a reporter for WNN.

My mouth opened and closed several times in an embarrassing display of... of... Well, I'm not sure what aspect of myself was on display, but it was not pretty, and would be analyzed and talked about ad-nauseam, and make it, in full color, onto the front of several tabloids. It is one of those moments I wish I could change. I wish I could go back in time and just keep walking. It would really have saved me a lot of embarrassment and heartache.

I finally tore my eyes away from her and moved into the empty parking area in front of the diner.

"Are you okay?" Lightningirl asked.

"Uh huh," I said. There I was with my own yes-no.

"What did she ask you?"

"If we were together."

Her eyes widened and she opened her mouth and closed it several times. I kind of expected the conversation to continue, but it didn't. She snapped her mouth closed and swiveled to the front door of Big Al's. "I think we should face him together."

Chapter 4

Introducing Toxicwasteman
Fall 2004, Green Valley, Arizona

Big Al's had a long counter you could eat at with round padded stools that swiveled on shining metal poles. It also had booth-style tables with high backs. I loved the place and wished I was just there for a burger.

Toxicwasteman was sitting on one of the stools slowly spinning himself around. The hostages, there were about a dozen of them, were all crowded behind the counter as far away from him as they could get.

I had seen pictures of him but had never seen him in person. It was clear he was a quantum-metamorph. So like I am a swirling yellow and Lightningirl is a blue-white, Toxicwasteman is a sickly green.

When we entered, he stopped his swiveling and faced us. I could see that the red vinyl of the seat was quickly eroding under his toxic touch. It smoked a bit when he stood up.

"Well, it's about time, isn't it?" he said.

Next to me Lightningirl was tense, and the lights flickered as she drew power from the place. I stepped forward in between the two of them and said, "So, I'm here, what do you want?"

"Oh," he said with a frown. "Not so quick. Let's not get right down to business. How about a little foreplay? After all, I've been stuck in prison for the last six months." He paused, looking me up and down and then doing the same to Lightningirl. His expression and the way his eyes lingered on my neutrino form making me very uncomfortable. "Does she know you're this quick?"

If I had been flesh and blood, I would have blushed, and I could feel Lightningirl bristling behind me. "What do you want?" I asked again, keeping my voice as even as possible.

He sighed and plopped himself back down on the stool. "Really? Are you really this much of a Boy Scout? No greeting to a fellow q-morph, no trading of superhero tips, no bragging about powers? Really? There just aren't many of us and it seems we ought to try to stick together. That's what I'm trying to do here."

"Excuse me?" I asked. I had no idea what he was talking about, what he meant by "trying to do here." Tom Tyree, Toxicwasteman, was a very smart guy, and I knew it. He wasn't some lowly flunky at the Hillington chemical plant when the accident happened--he was the chief scientist. He was one of those guys that were so smart that he could often be dumb (dumb in the ways of the normal mortals around him). So, when he didn't make sense, I assumed it was all about me. What I didn't know then was that he liked to mess with people. He liked to make them feel dumb.

He rolled his eyes, "Oh really? Well I'll spell it out. Look, I could have been in Mexico safely tucked away in a casita by the sea by now. All of this was to get you here, Mr. Neutrinoman."

Lightningirl stepped next to me, tendrils of electricity running down her extremities. I'm not sure where she drew all those watts from, but she was pretty lit up. "No Mexico for you. You're going right back to jail, if I have anything to do with it."

"Sweet, really," he said with a green-toothed smile and a dismissive wave of his hand. "Lovely, the two of you together are lovely. I think you'll live a long and happy life and have many super-babies, despite Mr. Neutrino's distaste for foreplay."

This was starting to annoy me. Why did everyone assume we were together? How could they tell? I sure as hell couldn't.

"But, darling," he continued, speaking to Lightningirl, "I've upped my game since we last met. I won't go down as easy a second time." He stood and cupped his right hand, a glowing ball of green goo forming in it. "One move from you, girly, and the hostages all die a terrible death."

I could see the reaction of the hostages behind him. They were cowering even farther back into the corner.

"You asked for me," I said, stepping in between them again. "So, what did you want to talk about?"

He sighed and plopped down on the disintegrating stool again, the green ball quickly diminishing in size until it was gone. "Oh yes, that. Well, you see--"

"First," I interrupted him, "let some of the hostages go."

He smiled, "You really are a Boy Scout, aren't you?"

"Hostages go before we talk."

He nodded, spinning himself around on the stool to face them. "In honor of our noble Neutrinoman, the women and children can go." He flipped his pulsing green hand from them towards the door as he spun back to face us, one leg crossed over the other.

Lightningirl and I moved aside, leaving the door clear as seven of the hostages left. An eighth, a young man, maybe twenty years old, tried to leave, but Toxicwasteman held out his arm and said, "Not you." The young man slunk back behind the counter. "Are you satisfied?" he asked me.

"Yes."

"Okay then. Here's the bullet, boys and girls. I know about the aliens. There are several species involved, and they call themselves the Arcturian Alliance. I know they knocked that asteroid out of orbit and aimed it at the Earth a few months ago, and I know you stopped it, saving us all." When he said, "saving us all," his hands rose up and flapped in front of him, his voice edged up half an octave.

"How do you know this?" Lightningirl asked.

"Why are you telling me this?" I asked.

"Well," he began, "I know this because they told me. I'm telling you this because their next plan to destroy us is nigh."

"Told you? Plan? Destroy us? Nigh?" I stammered.

"Yes, 'nigh,' as in here, upon us, about to happen."

"I know what 'nigh' means," I growled.

"Very well then, what was your question? I forgot it amidst all the stuttering."

"Why are you telling me?" I repeated.

"Because, this is my planet too, and I love it dearly." He crossed his hands over his heart, tilted his head and gave us a big smile. "Because, my dear Boy Scout, you are the only one that can stop them, again. Sorry darling," he said to Lightningirl, "a little lightning just ain't going to cut it."

"Why, I--" she began, as the lights began to flicker again.

"And," he continued, cutting her off, "because time is running out. Because we are the planet's only hope. Because I want to be one of the good guys this time. I want to be a hero."

Want more? The next episode of "Neutrinoman and Lightningirl: A Love Story," Toxic Asset, is available now! Go to Neutrinoman.com for the latest on the series.

Acknowledgements

Many thanks to my super team of Beta readers; you have made this a much better book: John Bifano, Roni Hornstein, Chris Kalinich, Peter Klein, Michele Lytle, Gary D. McClellan, Linda Robinson, Aleia N. O'Reilly, and Eliot Schipper.

Thanks to the amazing Diana Cox who proofread for me. If you want her on your team, you can email her at support@novelproofreading.com or visit her web page at www. novelproofreading.com.

The beautiful image of the Earth on the cover came from NASA's Visible Earth project. Check it out at: visibleearth. nasa.gov

I began this story by dedicating it to my wife, and I have to end it by thanking her. She has brought so much to my life and I am so grateful. Thanks for always being there.

And most of all, thank you for reading!

About the Author

ROBERT J. MCCARTER IS VERY COMFORTABLE WRITING about characters as long as one of those characters is not himself. Actually, Robert is anything but comfortable speaking (or writing) of himself in the third person—he finds it pretentious and silly.

So, let's drop all that usual bio crap.

Hi, my name is Robert, and I make things up and write them down. As a reader you may be interested in knowing something about me, so here goes:

I am a computer programmer by trade and have been for a very long time. I wrote my first program over thirty years ago and never stopped. I found the dramatic arts in high school, which got me through that rather daunting rite of passage, and fell in love with the arts. After high school, I started writing really bad poetry about how lonely I was and how clueless I was about the opposite sex (which, fortunately for all of us, I burned). After that my writing turned towards fiction.

I have written sporadically for several decades, and in what is, in all probability, part of a mid-life crisis, I started writing seriously (i.e. regularly) a few years ago. I have always been drawn to the arts (acting, photography, fractal art, and writing) and find that I am most happy when I am being as creative as possible. Thus, all the sitting alone at my computer making things up.

My writing is colored by my technical (i.e. geek) past as well as my age. I'm no youngster, so themes of death, grief, and change tend to creep into my writing (Okay, that's an understatement). Also, having been trained as an engineer, I like things to make sense and do my best to keep the hand waving to a minimum.

If you asked me to succinctly say something to summarize my writing style, I would tell you to go buzz off. But then, after profuse apologies, I would say: "I write humanist-geek, character-oriented sci-fi with heart."

I live in the middle of a Ponderosa Pine forest in the mountains of Arizona with my beautiful wife and my ridiculously adorable dog.

If you'd like to get a hold of me, use the contact form on my website (RobertJMcCarter.com/contact-me/). I'd love to hear from you, really I would.

Oh, and if you want the inside scoop on my writing, sign up for my newsletter (I won't share your name and emails are infrequent—around once a month). You can sign up using the blue box on the right of my website at RobertJMcCarter.com.

Books by Robert J. McCarter

Novels in the "Ghost's Memoir" world:
Shuffled Off: A Ghost's Memoir, Book 1
Drawing the Dead
To Be a Fool: A Ghost's Memoir, Book 2

Novellas (short novels) in the
Neutrinoman and Lightningirl Series:
Meteor Attack!
> Lightningirl and Neutrinoman, A Love Story. Episode 1

Toxic Asset
> Lightningirl and Neutrinoman, A Love Story. Episode 2

Protocol X
> Lightningirl and Neutrinoman, A Love Story. Episode 3

Season 1 (Omnibus edition of Episodes 1 - 3)
Off Book
> Lightningirl and Neutrinoman, A Love Story. Episode 4
> *(Coming soon)*

Novelettes
Probability: Resolve
The Turing Test Will Be Televised
Ghost Hacker, Zombie Maker

For a complete list, go to RobertJMcCarter.com

www.ingramcontent.com/pod-product-compliance
Lightning Source LLC
Chambersburg PA
CBHW030615130626
46552CB00002B/584